Olivia was still yawning as she left her house the next morning. Every time she'd fallen asleep last night, she'd been woken by memories of the spooky events at Café Creative. The strange girl in the red Victorian costume, the wind that had wailed through the room, slamming doors and giving everyone chills.

If the Halloween party's big finish hadn't been one of Camilla's planned effects, then who – or *what* – could have caused it?

Sink your fangs into these:

MY SISTER THE VAMPIRE

Switched

Fangtastic!

Revamped!

Vampalicious

Take Two

Love Bites

Lucky Break

Star Style

Twin Spins!

Date with Destiny

Flying Solo

Stake Out!

Double Disaster!

Flipping Out!

Secrets and Spies

Fashion Frightmare!

MY BROTHER THE WEREWOLF

Cry Wolf!

Puppy Love!

Howl-oween!

Tail Spin

Sienna Mercer

MY SISTER THE VAMPIRE

SPOOKTACULAR!

EGMONT

With special thanks to Stephanie Burgis

For Violet

EGMONT
We bring stories to life

My Sister the Vampire: Spooktacular! first published in
Great Britain 2015 by Egmont UK Limited, The Yellow Building,
1 Nicholas Road, London W11 4AN

Copyright © Working Partners Ltd 2015
Created by Working Partners Limited, London WC1X 9HH

ISBN 978 1 4052 7843 0

1 3 5 7 9 10 8 6 4 2

A CIP catalogue record for this title is available from the British Library

Typeset by Avon DataSet Ltd, Bidford on Avon, Warwickshire B50 4JH
Printed and bound in Great Britain by the CPI Group

60956/1

MIX
Paper
FSC FSC® C018306

Chapter One

Olivia Abbott was sitting next to her identical twin on the school bus, trying to memorise new lines for her upcoming movie, when she suddenly heard a squeal of excitement from across the aisle.

'Ooh, Olivia and Ivy, look at this!' Waving a magazine in the air, their friend Reiko reached over to nudge Olivia's shoulder. But from the super-strong pink-haired vampire exchange student, the "nudge" felt more like a shove.

'Careful!' laughed Ivy, as Olivia bounced off her shoulder. She looked over her twin's head at Reiko. 'What's up?'

'My horoscope!' Beaming, Reiko held up the teen magazine that she'd been reading. 'We don't get this magazine back in Japan. This is fangtastic!'

'Oh, honestly!' Ivy rolled her eyes. Unlike Reiko, who was dressed in eye-wateringly neon athletic gear, Ivy was a typical American vampire goth. Black kohl lined her eyes, and her long black hair streamed over the shoulders of her lacy black sweater. Slim black trousers and big black boots completed her ensemble, making her look even fiercer as she crossed her arms over her chest. 'You don't really believe in horoscopes, do you?'

'Well . . .' Reiko shrugged, her high ponytail bouncing above her lime-green tank top. 'Maybe not, but it's still fun to read them, isn't it? I love all the spooky warnings and weird pieces of advice. Check out *yours*!' She folded back the cover of the magazine, pointing at the page she was reading. '"Do not be confused by the mirror from the past. Listen for the wailing winds of memory".'

'"The wailing winds of memory"?' Olivia repeated. She scrunched her eyebrows together in thought as she twitched her rumpled silver skirt and pale pink sweater back into place. 'What could *that* mean?'

'It doesn't mean *anything*,' Ivy told her. 'Horoscopes are just superstition.'

'Maybe you're right,' Olivia said, 'but personally . . .' She gave her twin a meaningful grin. 'I've learned not to be too certain about anything these days.'

After all, there had been a time, not that long ago, when she thought the whole idea of vampires was "superstition". Now here she was, riding between two of them on her way to a traditional vampire celebration!

A *lot* of things had changed in the last year.

The bus was already slowing to a stop on Undertaker Hill, where Ivy lived with the twins' vampire bio-dad and step-mom. Olivia waited in the aisle as Ivy wrestled out a mysterious cardboard box that she had wedged under their seat when they first got on.

'Come on,' Olivia said as her twin finally straightened, holding the lid of the box firmly closed. 'Aren't you even going to give us a peek of what's inside that thing?'

'No way!' Ivy shook her head and started towards the door of the bus. Reiko followed right behind, the tennis racquet that was sticking out at a dangerous angle from her massive orange backpack nearly banging into Olivia. But even as Olivia hopped back to escape a concussion, she heard Ivy say: 'Trust me. You, of all people, do *not* want to see what's in this box! It's a Moonrise gift for Dad.'

Hmmm. It was the day before Halloween and they were on their way to the Vega house for the traditional vampire celebration of Moonrise. Olivia was pretty sure her sister was just trying to gross her out. *Well, joke's on you, twin. I'm not icked out by vampy things. Well, not as much as I used to be . . .*

She got out of the bus, and had to lurch backwards again to avoid bumping into Ivy, who had come to a sudden dead halt on the street.

'Oh no,' Ivy moaned, 'look who's heading straight for us!'

Reiko swung around. 'Who?'

As Olivia looked past the exchange student, she had to muffle a sigh of her own. Reiko might not recognise the pretty, preppy girl walking towards them – but for Olivia, the sight was all too familiar. 'It's Charlotte Brown,' she told Reiko. 'From our old middle school.' *And this is the worst possible time to meet her!* Olivia hoped that Charlotte wouldn't get nosy about what was in Ivy's box. *If there really is something super vampy in there, we can't let Charlotte see it!* Olivia might not bat an eyelid at vampy things these days, but Charlotte definitely would!

And they couldn't risk Charlotte seeing anything

that would make her suspicious. That would break the most important rule in the vampire world – that no non-vamps, or "bunnies" as they were known, could ever be allowed to discover that vampires really existed. As far as Olivia was aware, she was the only bunny in the world to know about the vamps, and only because she happened to be the identical twin sister of one!

'Hey, guys!' Charlotte beamed as she walked towards them. 'How *are* you? Looking forward to the party tomorrow?'

'Of course!' Olivia said brightly, still not used to the fact that the formerly mean head cheerleader was now one of the friendliest people she knew. 'We can't wait. We just know Camilla's going to give Café Creative the best Haunted House party ever!'

Charlotte gave a squeal of excitement as she clapped her hands together. 'Has Camilla given you any clues about what she's planned for it? She won't tell me anything!'

'You know Camilla . . .' Olivia shrugged, smiling.

Olivia's best friend, Camilla Edmunson, had taken charge of planning the first-ever Halloween party at Café Creative, the joint café and creative centre at the Franklin Grove Museum. And Camilla *always* went all-out on every project.

'She's keeping the details secret,' Olivia said, 'but everyone's talking about it. I'm sure it's going to be fabulous.'

'Of course it will! The school play she directed last year was really . . . memorable.'

Olivia's felt her cheeks flush, even as a smile tugged at her lips. *It was certainly memorable for me.* She'd had her first kiss onstage in *Romezog and Julietron.* Even better, it had been with her amazing movie-star boyfriend, Jackson Caulfield.

Charlotte was frowning, though, as she leaned forwards, dropping her voice to a whisper. 'To be honest, I'm just worried that the party might get too scary for me. Some of the rumours I've heard . . . well, do you think they're true? Would Camilla *really* create remote-controlled *zombies*?'

'Cool!' said Reiko, perking up.

'No!' said Ivy, rolling her eyes. 'Camilla's sure to give us all a few scares tomorrow, but she's not Doctor Frankenstein.'

'Whew.' Charlotte smiled and stepped back.

Reiko slumped. 'Too bad. Do you think there'll at least be a Frankenstein at the party, though?'

Ivy raised one eyebrow. 'Frankenstein's monster, you mean? Because you know, Frankenstein himself was –'

'I don't want to hear about it!' Charlotte said firmly. 'I'm already starting to feel S-I-A!'

Did anyone else understand that? Olivia turned to Ivy and Reiko, but they both shook their heads.

'S-I-*what*?' said Olivia.

Charlotte smiled proudly. 'I made it up myself,' she explained. '*Scared-In-Advance*. Get it?'

8

'Um . . . OK,' Olivia mumbled. *Somehow, I doubt that is going to catch on any time soon.*

Ivy coughed, starting to edge away. 'You know, we really need to hurry home, so . . .'

'Oh, sure, of course!' Charlotte bounced on her toes. 'But I'm just curious – what's in that box?'

Uh-oh, Olivia thought, desperately trying to think of a way of distracting Charlotte. But before she could, her twin sister piped up.

'Well actually, it's the reason we need to hurry. *Really* hurry,' Ivy said, 'because it's my Biology homework . . .' She raised the cardboard box and nodded meaningfully at the thin trail of red that was starting to trickle out of one bottom corner. '. . . and it could start getting *really smelly*, really soon. Trust me, you do not want to be here when that happens!'

'Eughh!' Charlotte lurched backwards, staring at the bright red droplets. 'Is that . . . blood?'

Ivy stepped closer, cracking open the lid of the

box as she lifted it towards Charlotte's face. 'Do you want to see it before I finish dissecting it?'

'*No!*' Charlotte stumbled back, staring in horror at the leaking red ooze. 'Actually, I . . . I think I'll just . . . see you guys at the party tomorrow! Bye!' She swallowed visibly, her face turning a sickly green as she spun around and hurried away. 'I am *so* glad I don't go to Franklin Grove High,' they heard her mumble. 'At least at my school, the homework is hygienic!'

Reiko clapped one hand to her mouth, barely muffling her laughter. Olivia waited until Charlotte was definitely out of hearing range before she turned to her twin, eyebrows raised. 'OK,' she said. 'You didn't actually bring a *dissection* as a Moonrise present for our dad . . . did you?'

'Sadly, no,' Ivy mocked disappointment. 'This was an assignment for Home Ec., not Biology. But I have to warn you, it's actually even scarier-looking than a dissection. There's no way I could have let Charlotte get a peek at it. See?' She lifted the lid of the box.

Olivia peered in – and giggled. Inside was the most lopsided mess of a cake she'd ever seen. Red jam was oozing everywhere.

Reiko lowered her hand and finally let her laughter tumble out. 'I think you need to put that cake out of its misery!'

Ivy shrugged. 'So I'm not the best baker in my family. Luckily, Dad is. Let's go celebrate Moonrise!'

Closing the lid of the cake box, she hurried up the steep hill to the Vegas' house, with Reiko close behind. Olivia followed, waiting for tension to fill her chest, for tingles of dread to flood her belly at the prospect of what their dad had planned for Moonrise.

Ivy opened the front door, which creaked loudly and ominously, and still Olivia waited for the moment she would feel officially creeped out. But it didn't come.

Am I . . . used to *spookiness now?*

As she stepped inside after her twin and Reiko, she took in a new, blood-red rug that lined the hallway. Her bio-dad, Charles Vega, usually decorated the house in classy shades of black and cream, but this rug's garish pattern of coffins and gravestones was definitely not part of that scheme.

It should have been spooky, but the only thing Olivia found "scary" about the rug was that it reminded her of the *really* frightening thing that was going on in her life right now: *Eternal Sunset,* the epic vampire romance movie she was shooting with her boyfriend Jackson. The latest rewrites were in, and that meant lots of new lines to learn, in a very short amount of time.

Fluffing my lines and looking like an idiot in front of our director: now that's scary! she told herself as she followed the others into the house. She closed the door behind her . . . and a blood-curdling shriek sounded from the kitchen.

What the . . .? Olivia's heart pounded in her chest as she headed towards the sound of the scream.

'Hey, give it back!' As the girls hurried into the kitchen, Olivia and Ivy's step-mom lunged forwards, grabbing for the bowl of cranberry sauce in her husband's hands. Lillian was usually the picture of flawless elegance, but today her sleek black dress was spattered with stains, and more crimson streaks covered her neck and face. 'I want to do the last step by myself!'

'Don't you dare!' Charles skipped backwards, his own tailored black suit just as dirty as Lillian's dress. He clutched the bowl to his chest with one hand while he flicked another messy handful of cranberry sauce at his wife. 'Back off! It's mine. You can have your turn next year!'

'Ugh!' With a cry of frustration, Lillian shook her sauce-covered hands at him, showering his whole outfit with globs of cranberry.

Seriously? Olivia turned to Ivy and Reiko in

wide-eyed wonder, her heart rate gradually returning to normal. *Are you seeing this, too?*

Ivy only shrugged, grinning. 'Things get a little different when it's Moonrise,' she whispered.

I'll say! Olivia thought. She giggled as she spotted a blood-red dot of cranberry sauce directly between her bio-dad's eyes. Of all the unlikely things in the world, she could never have imagined her super-formal bio-dad having a cranberry-sauce fight with his wife!

'Girls!' Charles looked up, finally taking notice of them. 'Oh, good, you're here just in time to see *me* finish off *my* perfect cranberry sauce.'

'Ohhh!' Lillian cast up her eyes in comic despair and turned away. 'I give up! You finish off the sauce. I'm going to prep the red velvet cake. Happy Moonrise, girls!'

'Happy Moonrise!' Olivia chorused right along with Ivy and Reiko.

Charles beamed as he began to stir the sauce.

14

'And now, just as we do every year, it's time to remember why this tradition was created in the first place.'

'How old is it, really?' Olivia asked, taking a seat at one of the tall stools by the breakfast bar.

Reiko sat down across from her, pulling out a tennis ball from her backpack and bouncing it from knee to knee as she listened.

'Moonrise? Oh, it's ancient!' Lillian answered, her voice muffled as she knelt down in front of the refrigerator to rummage through it.

'It is a very old vampire tradition,' Charles agreed, 'or at least . . . well, it's a very old *American* vampire tradition, anyway. I doubt it would ever happen back home.'

'Of course not.' Ivy rolled her eyes as she sat down next to Olivia. 'Transylvanian vampires are *way* too snooty for Moonrise.'

'Not Japanese vamps,' Rciko said cheerfully. 'We celebrate our own version of Moonrise, too.

And I've heard that in Kenya . . .'

'Ahem.' Charles fixed both girls with a stern look. It might have been more intimidating if half of his black hair hadn't been standing upright, the other half slicked back and sticky with cranberry sauce. '*As* I was saying . . . Moonrise is usually held on October 31st, the same day as Halloween. For bunnies, that date marks the end of the harvest season; for vampires, it signals the shift in power, when the moon dominates the day more than the sun.'

'But . . .' Olivia frowned. 'Real vampires don't need the moon. They can go out in the daytime just fine.'

'Of course we can.' Charles gave her a mischievous grin. 'But then, humans don't *need* to hunt Easter eggs or go trick-or-treating, do they? But they do it for fun.'

'And that's what Moonrise is all about,' Ivy said, bumping Olivia with her shoulder. 'Fun!'

16

Charles finished stirring the sauce and set his spoon aside. 'For obvious reasons, we've chosen to host our Moonrise get-together a day early this year. I knew you three wouldn't want to miss tomorrow's haunted house party.'

'Hey, it's not just them!' Lillian poked her head back out of the fridge for a moment, exposing her cranberry-stained cheeks. 'I'm looking forward to the party, too! I am still in charge of Café Creative, you know.'

'Not when it comes to *this* party,' Ivy told her. 'Tomorrow, it's Commander Camilla all the way!'

'Good point,' Lillian chuckled, ducking back into the fridge. 'I think you girls will be in for a treat – for a bunny, Camilla sure knows her way around a good scare!'

'Never mind. Tonight is all about Moonrise.' Charles opened a high cupboard and pulled out three coffin-shaped boxes: one black, one bright orange and one pale pink. 'One for each of you this year!' he said.

'Let me take a wild guess.' Olivia gave her bio-dad a teasing smile. 'Mine's the pink one?'

'Who else?' Ivy said, grinning. She grabbed the black box and pulled it open. 'Ooh!' A tombstone-shaped grey cookie lay inside, surrounded by a dusting of chocolate. 'It looks just like it's covered in dirt from a graveyard,' she said happily. 'Perfect!'

Reiko let out a delighted giggle when she opened her bright orange coffin. 'I love it!' She pulled out a little liquorice bat.

Is that actually . . . wriggling? Olivia laughed as Reiko popped a bat wing into her mouth.

The doorbell rang, and Ivy slid off her stool. 'I'll get that. But go ahead and open yours, sis!'

'OK.' Olivia saw her bio-dad's eager gaze, and wondered what kind of vampy gift went well with a *pink* coffin.

Of course, she thought, as she opened the box

and saw the pink candy heart waiting inside. But it wasn't a regular candy heart. This candy heart was shaped like a *real* heart – with valves and everything!

Seriously? Olivia giggled, and then had to stop herself from shaking her head in disbelief – not at the gift, but at herself. There was a time when this candy treat would have sent her running all the way home. But now, she was laughing in absolute delight!

She looked up at her bio-dad. A year ago, she'd barely known him. Now, he'd gone out of his way to try to choose the perfect gift for his human daughter. How could she not be touched?

She opened her mouth to thank him . . . but before she could say a single word, *another* ear-piercing scream ripped through the air.

It was coming from the hallway.

Ivy couldn't help shrieking at the sight before her. *Am I seeing things?* she wondered.

Standing in the front doorway was a girl wearing a fitted black jacket, long, narrow scarf, pencil skirt and high-heeled boots. Her black hair was longer than when Ivy had last seen it, the very tips still pixie-blonde from a rebellious dye-job the month before. 'I can't believe you're here!' Ivy cried. She threw her arms around her fashionista best friend, Sophia. 'Aren't you supposed to still be in Japan, finishing up your exchange programme? Reiko isn't flying back till next week.'

Sophia hugged her back tightly, and Ivy caught a whiff of an exotic new perfume. 'My parents decided they didn't want me away from home on Moonrise.'

'Yeah, right.' Grinning, Ivy released her friend and closed the front door to keep out the chilly late-October air. 'Come on, admit it. You were just too homesick to stay away!'

'Well, obviously.' Sophia rolled her eyes as she started towards the kitchen. 'Japan was just soooo

20

boring, what with all its incredible sights, cool people and amazing fashion . . . how could I *not* want to get back to sleepy little Franklin Grove as quickly as possible?'

'Ha!' Following Sophia into the kitchen, Ivy was still laughing at her friend's comeback even as Olivia let out a delighted shriek of her own.

'Sophia!' Olivia jumped off her stool to hug the new arrival. 'Welcome home!'

As Reiko stood up too, Ivy gestured towards her. 'Oh, and I should introduce . . .'

'No, I've got this.' Smiling, Sophia turned to Reiko. '*Hajimemashite,*' she said. '*Watashi wa Sophia to moushimasu.*'

Reiko beamed. '*Reiko desu. Yoroshiku!*'

'Wow.' Ivy blinked at her best friend. 'You really have learned Japanese!'

Sophia winced. 'Well, I'm not that good . . .'

'You're great!' Reiko insisted.

'You have to tell us all about your trip, Sophia,'

Lillian said, pulling out a stool for Sophia to sit on.

'Tell us about the food . . .' Charles licked his lips as he put cling film over his bowl of cranberry sauce. 'It's been so long since I've had any decent *udon* noodles!'

'Well, I want to hear about what you *saw*,' Olivia said. 'Tell me all about the fashion!'

'And the movies!' Lillian added. 'Can you believe the new Koizumi film won't be released here until January? You have to tell me all about it!'

Reiko shook her head. 'Before anything else, I need to know . . .' She fixed Sophia with an intent gaze. '. . . is my friend Megumi still dating that creep Tetsuo?'

A smile played over Sophia's lips as she leaned closer to Reiko. 'Actually, the day I left, Megumi was preparing for a very hot date . . . *with* . . .' Her words trailed off.

'With who? With who?' Reiko bounced on the edge of her seat.

'. . . Kaneda!' Sophia finished triumphantly.

'Yes!' Reiko pumped one arm in victory. 'I always thought he'd be so much better for her!'

Ivy had no idea who they were talking about, but she grinned along with them.

'Aha!' Sophia spun around, pointing an accusatory finger at Ivy. 'Gotcha! I caught you smiling. The Happy Vampire is back!'

'Augh!' Ivy groaned as the rest of her family burst into laughter. 'Don't remind me.' She had only just stopped having nightmares about the mix-up the twins had had at Café Creative's recent fashion show, when she and Olivia had accidentally ended up in each other's outfits. It wouldn't have been a problem – except that, as identical twins, the girls looked so similar that the vampire community had assumed that it was Ivy in the goth-tastic black gown, grinning like she'd just won a backstage pass to a Pall Bearers show.

'Well, as long as you aren't going to scare me

by smiling *all* the time . . .' Sophia teased. 'Because that would be too terrifying! I really –'

But Ivy didn't catch the rest of Sophia's sentence. Olivia's cell phone trilled loudly. Olivia pulled it out, opened up her text messages . . . and gasped.

'It's an SOS,' she said. 'Camilla needs our help with the set-up for tomorrow's party . . . otherwise she says it might be ruined!'

'Not if we can help it,' Ivy said. 'Come on, guys. We need to get to Café Creative, *now*!'

Chapter Two

T wenty minutes later, Olivia scrambled out of her bio-dad's sleek black car with a sigh of relief. It had never felt small to her before, but squeezing four girls inside had been a bit much!

As she stretched out her cramped arms and legs, she looked up at the sprawling building in front of her. Franklin Grove Museum loomed against the darkening sky, massive and Gothic, with big stone turrets rising towards the clouds. It was closed for the day, but the South Wing – where Café Creative was located – would be opening later. Ivy, Reiko and Sophia were all already hurrying up the stairs towards the great oak door, but Olivia hesitated.

'Dad?' She turned back and peered into the low-slung car, where Charles sat waiting to drive back home to Lillian. 'I hope . . . I mean, are you really OK with this? I know we were supposed to be helping you prepare for the Moonrise, and –'

'Don't worry.' Charles smiled up at her. 'Your loyalty to your friend is a great quality. I couldn't be more proud that both of my daughters naturally have it. And anyway . . .' he wiggled his eyebrows, '. . . there's still plenty of time to celebrate Moonrise when you get back!'

Uh-oh. As Olivia watched him drive off, she wondered about the gleam she'd spotted in his eye . . . and what it might mean about his plans for the rest of the Moonrise celebrations. *Something elaborate, no doubt,* she thought. *If I know my bio-dad!*

Ivy's voice broke through her thoughts. 'Come on, Olivia!' The three vampires were standing at the top of the stairs, looking down at her. 'Camilla said she needed us *now.*'

'Coming!' Olivia called back, hurrying up the stairs as quickly as her cute little ankle-boots would let her.

The other girls shuffled aside, making way for her in front of the big brass door knocker. Ivy cleared her throat. 'Um, we thought . . . well, why don't *you* knock for Albert?'

'Me?' Olivia took a quick step back. 'Why me?'

Ivy grimaced. Reiko turned away, whistling innocently as she bounced her tennis ball off the stone wall. Sophia looked faintly amused.

'I don't believe this,' Olivia said. She put her hands on her hips and did her best to give them a death-squint . . . even though she was pretty sure it was coming out as a half-smile. 'Just look at you guys! Three big, scary vampires – intimidated by a cranky old museum caretaker.'

'We're not *scared* of him, obviously,' Ivy mumbled. 'But . . . well, he won't scowl too much at *you*, right? I mean, you're so nice. And human.'

'That's never stopped him before,' Olivia muttered. But she took a deep breath and lifted the door knocker anyway . . . then winced as it slammed back against the oak door with a deafening sound.

The truth was, the museum's live-in caretaker really *was* intimidating. As a vampire, Albert had had more than a century to perfect his unimpressed glare. He might be good enough friends with her bio-dad to call him "Chas", but Olivia had never managed to really relax around him. *Just remember,* she told herself, *he's actually really nice. Probably. Maybe . . .*

'Ahhh!' She let out a muffled shriek and leaped back as the door opened to reveal . . . a vampire!

Or rather, a caretaker dressed exactly how bunnies *imagined* vampires looked.

'I beg your pardon,' Albert said stiffly, as Olivia caught her breath. His words lisped slightly over the long false fangs that stuck out of his mouth, above streaks of painted blood that ran down his chin like red lightning. His face looked even paler than usual when framed by his cape's upturned black collar, which looked rather like bat wings . . . but apparently nothing could change his bored expression, not even his current outfit. 'Miss Edmunson felt I needed to . . . *rehearse* my role for tomorrow night's performance.'

'Rehearse?' Sophia asked. She raised one eyebrow.

Albert's jaw set, and his voice lowered to a gruff mutter. 'She said . . . that I was not a very convincing vampire.'

As Olivia stared at him, open-mouthed, she heard Reiko make a choking sound. From the corner of her eye she saw Sophia turn away, her shoulders quivering. Ivy clamped one hand to her mouth, her face bright red. *Uh-oh,* Olivia thought. *If they can't hold themselves back . . .*

One more look at the plastic vampire teeth

poking out of Albert's mouth had Olivia bursting into laughter right along with the three vamp girls, the last of her nerves sliding away.

For the first time that Olivia could remember, Albert actually cracked a smile. 'Go along,' he said, and waved at the dimly-lit corridor behind him.

Then he turned around with a *swish* of his flowing cloak, striding away before they could say another word.

Shadows loomed from every corner as they hurried down the corridor, but Olivia ignored them. She was used to the gloomy museum atmosphere at night.

'That was so funny,' Ivy sniggered. 'I wonder if Albert – *wahhh*!' Letting out a sudden shriek, she jumped into Olivia's arms, clinging on like a frightened monkey.

Olivia laughed as she looked up and saw the creature whose legs must have brushed against Ivy's head in the dark.

It was a giant mummy puppet dangling from the ceiling, limp and saggy.

'I think you're safe now,' Olivia said wryly. She patted Ivy's shoulder. 'All it can really do is kick you, right?'

'What?' Blinking, Ivy turned her face up to look. Then she let out an embarrassed groan, jumping down to the ground and brushing herself off. 'I can't believe I did that!'

'I'm glad you did,' said Olivia. 'You beat me to it. I hate things that make me jump. Now we're both scaredy-cats!'

'Shouldn't that be "scaredy-bats"?' said Reiko.

'Oh, I love it!' Sophia clapped her hands as she stepped up beside them. 'I've been waiting my entire life for Ivy to have a scaredy-bat moment!'

'All right, enough already!' Ivy rolled her eyes and stomped off down the hall ahead of them, her big black boots clomping against the marble floor.

31

'Watch out for any more terrifying monsters up there!' Olivia called after her. 'Just remember, I'm right here to protect you!'

'Ha, ha, ha. Very funny!' Ivy called back. 'But I warn you: I'll aim death-squints at every one of you if you keep this up any longer!'

Still grinning, Olivia hurried after her sister. As they turned another corner in the twisting corridor, though, a portrait that she had never seen before caught her eye and made her turn her head to look even as she kept moving.

Ooh, more twins! In the picture, two girls who looked about the same age as herself and Ivy sat next to each other, both dark-haired, holding hands, their identical faces alight with beaming smiles. Their floor-length, wide-skirted dresses billowed out around them, and their hair was done up in elaborate ringlets that fell around their faces. Based on their outfits, which looked kind of like the ones Olivia wore for *Eternal Sunset*, she guessed that the girls must have been painted at least a hundred and fifty years ago. *Mental note to show this to Ivy on our way out!*

Olivia turned her gaze back to the corridor ahead – and screamed. A giant alien loomed over her, tentacles raised as if to attack.

'Ahhhhh!' She leaped forwards and latched on to her twin in a panicked piggyback.

Ivy didn't even break her stride. But she shook her head as Sophia and Reiko's laughter filled the corridor behind them. 'Camilla strikes again!' Ivy said ruefully.

Olivia raised her head to peek back over her shoulder. Then she flopped against her sister's back in relief. 'Oh . . . it was just a dummy!'

'Of course,' Sophia said cheerfully. 'Camilla's training to be a movie director, remember? She's good at creating "atmosphere"!'

'I almost wish she wasn't,' Olivia mumbled, as she dropped off her sister and back on to the floor.

Ivy gave her an "I-told-you-so" look. 'Not so funny now, is it?'

'Well . . .' Olivia smoothed down her clothes, wanting to change the subject. 'I just wonder where she got all these props!'

They passed another five scary dummies before they finally came to the doors of Café Creative.

'If the path to the café is that good,' Reiko said, her eyes gleaming, 'what do you think it's like *inside*?'

'I guess we'll find out.' Bracing herself, Olivia pushed open the door to the brightly-lit open space at the front of Café Creative.

Well, it was *usually* an open space. Today, the whole area in front of the café tables was covered in a humongous pile of raggedly-dressed, decomposing zombie bodies. *Ewww!* Olivia shuddered despite herself.

OK, she was pretty sure that those were just mannequins, along with some old clothes stuffed

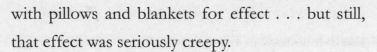

with pillows and blankets for effect . . . but still, that effect was seriously creepy.

And where was Camilla, anyway?

'Camilla?' Olivia called out tentatively, stepping into the room. Her voice echoed off the walls and the dark windows.

'Mmmmfff!' A muffled answering cry sounded.

Olivia frowned, turning to search for the source of the sound, but the other three girls, with their vampiric super-hearing, were already hurrying forwards.

'She's buried underneath that pile!' Ivy said, pointing at the zombie hill.

'Oh, great.' Olivia sighed as she started forwards. 'I never planned to get this up close and personal with a zombie!'

Working together, the four girls dug through the "bodies" until Camilla's head finally popped out from underneath a zombie.

'Whew!' She took a deep breath, her blonde

curls shaking wildly around her face. 'It feels like I've been stuck in there forever!'

Olivia took one of Camilla's arms while Ivy took the other, helping their friend out from underneath the last few zombies that had pinned down her legs. 'How did this happen?' Olivia asked.

'Oh, you know . . .' Camilla leaned back down to dig through the zombies. A moment later, she pulled out her purple beret, wiped off a fleck of "brain" and plopped it back on top of her curls. 'There was a bit of a domino situation when I was repositioning these guys,' she explained. 'I called and called to Albert, but . . .' She shrugged. 'He must have been on the other side of the building, because he didn't hear me. That's why I had to text you for help.'

'Umm . . .' Olivia shared a look with the three vampires and saw that they were thinking the same thing as her.

With Albert's super-hearing, he *must* have heard

Camilla's cry for help. The fact that he had chosen not to respond to it . . . well, as much as Olivia loved her friend, she knew exactly how intense Camilla could get when she was in directing mode. And she could only imagine how little the old vampire enjoyed being directed!

'Never mind,' Olivia said briskly. 'Now that we're here, we can help you set up the rest of the zombies so you don't have any more accidents on your own.'

'That would be *fabulous*.' Camilla stepped back and framed the scene with her hands as if she were looking at it all through a camera lens. 'I want it to feel like they're actually guests *at* the party. So I need one of them by the café counter, another few sitting at tables with knives and forks in their hands . . .'

Ivy leaned over and scooped up a gruesome zombie body, letting it dangle over her arm without so much as a wince of disgust. 'Let's get started!' she said cheerfully.

As all four girls set to work under Camilla's direction, Olivia forced herself to ignore the leaking brains of the zombie bodies they were working with, even when Camilla pointed to the worst one Olivia had seen yet.

'Could you take that one over to the far table?' Camilla asked.

'Of course.' Pinning a weak smile to her face, Olivia pulled the "zombie" off the pile. The mannequin's eyes were a creepy shade of yellowish-orange.

Olivia took deep, calming breaths as she carried the mannequin all the way across the room. She sat it down at the table, taking her time to position its arms as if it were actually eating a meal. *I'm tough Olivia now, not bunny Olivia any more. Remember? And I know exactly how to follow a director's orders.*

Then her cell phone's ringtone burst out inside her handbag, and she nearly leaped out of her skin. 'Ahh!'

'Ha!' Ivy shook her head and pointed at Olivia as the other girls' laughter echoed around the room. 'You're losing two-to-one on the scaredy-bat score now!'

'Hmmph.' Olivia pulled out her still-ringing cell phone and gave her twin a mock-annoyed look.

Then she saw the picture on her cell phone, and her lips curved into a smile.

There was no way to get real privacy with three vampires in the room, but she moved away a few more feet and turned her back to the others as she answered her boyfriend's call. 'Hey, you! How are you doing?'

'I'm fine.' Jackson's voice wrapped warmly around her. 'I just wanted to give you a heads-up. Have you checked your email yet?'

Olivia laughed. 'I've kind of had my hands full. Literally! I've been hauling zombies around for Camilla's Halloween party.'

'Really?' Jackson paused. '*You?*'

'Don't sound so surprised!' Olivia said with mock-outrage. 'I'm not a bu– I mean, I'm a tough girl now. Anyway – what email?'

'Well . . .' Jackson sighed. 'All those scenes we're shooting in Pine Wood in a couple of weeks have just been rewritten – again.'

'Oh no!' Squeezing her eyes shut, Olivia rubbed her temple with her free hand, trying to massage away a sudden headache. 'So we have *new* dialogue to memorise now? I was just getting the first pages down. I've practically been monologuing in my sleep!'

'Oh, yeah?' She heard a hint of amusement in Jackson's voice. 'So, how's your Southern accent coming along?'

Olivia grinned as she turned back towards the Halloweenified Café Creative, where Camilla was still busy directing and the three vampire girls had their faces politely turned away from Olivia and her conversation. Putting on her best Southern accent, she declared, 'Ah think it's gettin' bettah, sugah!'

All three vamp girls swung towards her.

Ivy's eyes were wide with horror. Sophia cringed, looking pained. Reiko only shook her head sadly.

Uh-oh. Olivia winced.

Maybe she needed a little more practice after all!

🦇　　　🦇　　　🦇

Ivy was still yawning after school the next day as she sat at her computer, wearing her Halloween costume and cycling through the photos from last night's Moonrise party. It hadn't started until they'd gotten back from Café Creative, and it hadn't ended until well after midnight, but it had totally been worth the sleep loss.

Just look at Olivia going vamp-y! In the first few photos, Olivia was holding up and then eating one of a dozen heart-shaped biscuits smothered in cranberry sauce, which Charles had made especially for her. In the next four photos, Ivy had captured her twin making funny faces with the sauce dripping from both sides of her mouth, just like a movie vampire.

We really did vamp-i-fy her!

A thump from downstairs signalled the front door opening and closing. Her step-mom's voice sounded a moment later, calling up the stairs.

'Reiko's on her way to see you, Ivy!'

Fangtastic! Ivy jumped off her chair, straightening her costume with the help of the mirror that hung on her closet door. *When Reiko sees this, she is so totally going to freak out!*

The door burst open, and Reiko strode in . . . only to stop, staring, as the door slammed shut behind her. 'Oh, *wow.*' She looked Ivy up and down, shaking her head in wonder. 'You are rocking that Sherlock Holmes costume!'

'Thank you!' Holding on to her deerstalker, Ivy gave a twirl so that her tweed cape swirled around her. 'I thought it was perfect for an investigative-journalist-in-training. Now . . . what are *you*?' She studied Reiko, tilting her head to take in every detail of the neon-green dress that reached down almost to Reiko's knees – but half of it was completely hidden by the rest of her costume. Rusted metal covered Reiko's left arm and leg, and half her chest; the left half of her hair had been dyed silver to match. 'Some kind of rusty droid, maybe? Or . . .' Ivy frowned as she took in the other, jet-black half of Reiko's hair, and her non-metallic right side. '. . . *half* a rusty droid?'

'Exactly!' Reiko swung an imaginary tennis racquet, then flung up her arm as if she'd scored a point. 'I'm Kumiko!'

Ivy shook her head as she sank back down on to her chair in front of the computer. 'Kumik-*who*?'

'You know!' Reiko rolled her eyes. 'The half-robot, half-human main character from *Droid Town*? It's one of the most popular manga comics in Japan!'

'Um . . . OK.' As the front door opened and

closed again downstairs, Ivy sighed. 'You look great,' she told Reiko, 'but you might want to prepare for a lot of people at tonight's party not knowing who you've come as.'

Reiko snorted, waving at her outfit. 'Come on, Sherlock. Who else could I possibly be, when I'm dressed like this?'

Ivy shrugged. 'They'll probably think you're something from *Star Wars*.'

Reiko's mouth dropped open in outrage and Ivy giggled.

She realised that she was really going to miss Reiko when she went home, even with Sophia back now. It was a shame that Sophia wasn't coming to the party, but Ivy understood that her parents wanted a family Moonrise after their daughter had been away for so long.

'OK, Kumiko, are your, uhm . . . batteries charged?' Ivy asked, grinning.

Reiko closed her eyes and made a *whirring* noise.

44

Then she spoke in a cute, robotic drone: 'System analysis reports that battery is at one hundred percent capacity, Mr Holmes!'

🦇　　　🦇　　　🦇

Half an hour later, Ivy gave Olivia's hand a squeeze as they walked with Reiko up to the doorway to the museum. 'I can tell you're not worried about walking this corridor again.'

Her twin smiled at her. 'That doesn't mean I'm *looking forward* to it, though.'

Ivy gave her a nudge, pointing at her pale pink witch costume. 'Besides, you've got the scariest outfit!'

'Ha ha.' Olivia rolled her eyes, but her lips twitched. 'Just because you have an unnatural fear of the colour pink . . .' She squeezed Ivy's hand and started forwards.

Ivy wasn't about to be taken off guard again the way she had been last night. *No more bunny hops for me!* Still, she couldn't help but be impressed by

Camilla's skill as the girls had to dodge shuffling zombies, groaning ghosts and bandaged mummies. Luckily, the models were all on just the right side of "too scary" . . .

Well, except for those five! Models don't breathe . . . or stink. Camilla definitely didn't put these ones here!

Ivy narrowed her eyes, using her vampire super-sight to pick out the five boys huddled together in the shadows of the next room, still as statues, obviously waiting to jump out and scare them.

'Come on, Josh,' she yelled. She would have recognised the closest as the meanest boy in their high school by his repulsive stench, even if she hadn't had vamp-vision. 'Don't you have anything better to do? You're not even in costume!'

'Oh, yeah?' Shaking back his lank hair, Josh stalked forwards, his long, leather trenchcoat swishing around him. From the smirk on his face, he wasn't even the slightest bit put out by being recognised. And he wasn't ready to back down, either.

Ivy crossed her arms, giving him a death-squint. *Unbelievable.* His hair had somehow managed to achieve an even greater state of "greasy" than it ever had before.

'What do you think, guys?' Josh asked his cronies as they emerged from the shadows behind him. 'Do we have somewhere better to be? Or would we rather stay . . . right . . . here?'

The boy just behind him gave a snort of laughter, and Ivy's eyes widened.

Uh-oh. This, she hadn't expected. It looked like Josh's new main henchman was Garrick Stephens. She hadn't seen him since he'd started at the other high school in town, but he had been the head "Beast" at Franklin Grove Middle School, his gang of vamp boys all doing their best to make every other kid in school miserable.

'I've been hearing stories about you from my crew,' Josh told Ivy, his smirk widening. He looked her up and down, then said to Garrick, 'So, this was the girl you kissed in the school play last semester?'

'Nope.' Garrick gave a goofy grin as he pointed straight to Olivia. 'It was the other one.'

'*Int-er-est-ing*,' Josh drawled. His eyes gleamed dangerously as he turned to Olivia.

'Hey!' Ivy sidestepped to stand protectively in front of her twin, but Olivia quickly stepped around her, face scrunched up in outrage.

'I did *not* kiss Garrick!' she declared. 'Camilla's script for *Romezog and Julietron* said I was *supposed* to kiss him as part of the play, but . . .' She glared at Garrick, who was still grinning at her. '. . . thankfully he had to run offstage early in the performance because he'd gone off-script!'

'That's right,' Ivy said. 'Plus, he was itching all through the whole show!' She gave Josh a smirk, hoping that it looked just as rude as the one he'd been aiming at her sister. 'But then, you probably get that, too, don't you? You seem to have the same lax approach to personal hygiene.'

'Ha!' Josh snickered, turning to Garrick. 'You got put in your place, dude.'

'Aw, Josh . . .'

Seriously? Ivy stared at the head of the greasy gang. *You didn't even notice that I was insulting you, too?*

'Come on.' Josh jerked his head towards the South Wing of the museum, where the party was waiting. 'We've got cooler places to be. But you . . .' His gaze landed on Ivy, and his face hardened. Suddenly, Ivy was very certain that he *had* noticed her insult . . . and would remember it. 'Don't worry . . . I'll be seeing *you* again.'

He started for the café, his dirty leather coat crackling with every movement.

Ivy let her held breath out in a whoosh of relief as the four other boys followed after him and finally disappeared from view, leaving the three girls alone in the darkened corridor. As she turned back to her friends, though, they shared a long look. She knew they were all thinking the same thing:

Garrick the Beast has found a buddy even meaner than him. We should probably steer clear . . . Which is not going to be a problem.

Oh my darkness, do they smell terrible!

Chapter Three

'Ugh!' Olivia cringed as the zombie mannequin at her table fell against her *again,* knocking her candy apple into her chest before she could take a bite. Caramel smeared all over the front of her dress as she heaved the bulky mannequin back into place, its yellowish-grey eyes staring sightlessly at her.

'You're not even gross any more,' she muttered, giving the mannequin one last shove. 'You're just irritating! You ruined my outfit!'

Then she looked up and gave a start of surprise as she saw a girl sitting opposite her at the small table, wearing a fabulous, deep-red Victorian-style dress that put Olivia's pink caramel-smeared witch costume to shame. *I must have been more distracted than I'd realised. I didn't even hear her arrive!* Instead of facing Olivia, the girl sat sideways on her seat, her wide hooped skirts spread around her and her eyes darting around the crowded dance floor, watching the rest of the party guests moving and mingling through Café Creative. Her hands were clenched around something in her lap.

'Hi!' Olivia said. Then she winced as she realised that the new girl must have heard her talking to the zombie mannequin. 'Sorry, my, uh, "boyfriend" is being a little annoying tonight,' she joked.

The other girl turned away without a word, angling herself towards the dance floor so that all Olivia could see was her back.

Ouch. Olivia gave up. *She's obviously waiting for someone . . . but seriously, would it hurt for her to just be a little friendly in the meantime?*

Sighing, she set down her uneaten apple and

looked out across the café at her own friends. Reiko was trying to teach Ivy how to robot dance and it wasn't going very well. Ivy looked stiff even by robot standards!

Olivia was so glad for Camilla's sake that the party was going so well. Café Creative was crammed to bursting, and Olivia recognised students from both her own school and Willowton High filling the dance floor and the tables. Her friends Finn and Amelia – or "Famelia", as Olivia preferred to call them – were dancing together in the centre of the room. Finn was dressed as a zombie surfer, while Amelia was her usual goth self. *I'm not sure Amelia's even in costume,* Olivia thought. *But it hardly matters when you're as fabulous as she is!*

Closer to the wall, Penny Taylor, the ex-goth, was looking utterly adorable in bright blue fairy wings as she laughed up at her own boyfriend, Maxie, who was dressed as a superhero. Lillian stood near the back as a chaperone, looking elegant and fabulous in a slinky black dress, with a long white streak sprayed into her black hair.

The only empty area that Olivia could spot in the room was . . . *oh, yuck*. She grimaced as she saw Josh Dillon having way too much fun dancing with one of the zombie mannequins while his followers cheered him on. *No wonder the other guests are trying to keep their distance!*

Still, she had to give him one tiny piece of credit: he could actually waltz surprisingly well!

Thump! The mannequin fell on top of her again, and Olivia groaned. This time, though, when she shoved it off, she found the girl opposite leaning across the table, looking straight at Olivia and clutching a large, striking bracelet made of chunky black stones.

'Have you seen Hope?' the girl asked urgently.

Oh, what a perfect Southern accent! Olivia felt a pang of excitement as she heard the other girl's drawl. *Maybe if I help her find this Hope girl, she'll help me with my accent for the movie!*

Olivia pushed the mannequin back into its chair with a grunt of effort. 'I'm sorry,' she said to the girl. 'I don't know anyone named Hope – but honestly, I don't know many people from Willowton. That must be where you go to school, right?'

Before the girl could answer, the mannequin slipped back out of its chair, heading directly towards Olivia.

Not again! Gritting her teeth, Olivia fought it back into place, then looked back to the girl . . .

Seriously? Olivia stared at the now-empty chair. *Talk about rude! And besides . . .* She frowned as she looked around the crowd. *How did she even get away so quickly? It's like she vanished into thin air!*

Oh well. She sighed and gave the mannequin a warning look as it started to slide again. 'You might be the friendlier of my two neighbours at this table,' she told him. 'But I'd rather be ignored by that girl all night than pick you up again!'

A loud clap of thunder suddenly echoed through Café Creative, cutting off the pounding dance music. The lights flickered, then disappeared, turning the room dark for one pulsating moment. Gasps and screams sounded across the café.

And then the lights flicked back on – just in time for a swarm of ghosts to come screaming through the air, swooping down low over all the party guests' heads.

'Ahhh!' Olivia ducked reflexively, her heartbeat speeding up. She heard startled laughter all around, though, and it was enough to make her look twice at the ghost that had nearly landed on her.

It's made of gauze, she realised, *and . . . wait. I know those curtains!* She had seen them hanging in Camilla's living room. Now that Olivia wasn't so taken aback, she could even make out the elaborate wires that had swung the ghosts from the ceiling.

She started to relax . . . a moment too soon.

Something long and rubbery landed on her shoulder.

'Auggh!' Olivia barely even noticed she was clutching at the zombie mannequin. She didn't care. She just needed something safe to cling on to!

Shrieks sounded throughout the room, all laughter replaced by panic.

Why, why, why wouldn't Camilla give me a heads-up on what to expect? Then I could have prepared myself! Olivia leaned back in her chair as massive black spiders suddenly dropped down on to the table in front of her, moving around with scuttles so horribly realistic that she found herself scooting even closer to the mannequin, until she was nearly sitting in its lap. *Being startled every five seconds is* not *fun!*

She wished *so much* that Ivy was here instead of halfway across the room doing the robot!

A wave of nervous but excited chatter swept across the room as the party finally resumed, the dance music blasting back over the loudspeakers.

Olivia focused on taking deep breaths, trying to force her heartbeat to return to normal.

It's all over. It's all o—

'Aahh!' Despite herself, she let out one last shriek as a hand landed on her arm.

'Hey, it's only me!' Grinning, Ivy slid into the seat across from her. 'But you'd better look out . . .' She pointed to the mannequin that Olivia was clutching. 'The last thing you want is for the paparazzi to see this. Jackson's fans will turn on you in an instant if they think you're cheating on him with Zombie Zach!'

Olivia flushed with embarrassment as she realised just how tightly snuggled up she was to the disgusting mannequin. 'Eww!' she cried, and gave it a hard shove.

Zombie Zach landed unceremoniously on the ground, his legs and arms sprawled crookedly against the floor.

'Aw.' Ivy clucked her tongue. 'Come on, buddy.

Just because you got dumped, you don't have to look so sad! I'd dance with you.'

'Like Josh was doing?' Grimacing, Olivia looked out over the crowd. 'At least I can't see him any more.'

Ivy snorted. 'His whole gang probably fled in terror when Camilla's show started up. Typical boys!' She took a large bite of candy apple and gave Olivia a pleading look. 'Please come with me on a tour of the room? Let's see all of the amazing effects that our brilliant friend put together!'

Olivia feigned confusion. 'So, you don't want to do the robot with Reiko any more?'

Ivy scooped her magnifying glass out of her pocket, extending it to Olivia. 'Guess I'm not the only detective in the family! Come on – before Kumiko's batteries have recharged!'

'Well, OK then, Miss Holmes. Let's go!' Despite herself, Olivia laughed and got up with Ivy.

Sidestepping dancing couples and zombies with

their rotting arms outstretched, Olivia followed her twin around the edges of the dance floor, passing witches and wizards, orcs and elves, and three Katnisses from *The Hunger Games*. 'There really are a lot of great costumes here,' she said as she passed a perfect Peeta. 'I like that one over th– ahh!' She sucked in a breath as a blurred shape flitted past her. 'What was that?'

'What?' Ivy turned around, laughing. 'Are you imagining things now? Halloween really *has* spooked you!'

'I didn't imagine it, I swear! It was so fast, it looked like a ghost, or . . .' Olivia's voice cut off into a squeak as the shape blurred past her again, this time moving in the opposite direction.

'Hmm.' Ivy's eyes narrowed as she tracked the blurred figure with her gaze. 'OK, you're not imagining this one. But trust me, that's no ghost . . . and you have nothing to worry about.'

'Huh?' Olivia blinked.

But before she could ask her twin for an explanation, the shape whizzed towards them again, superhumanly fast . . . then came to a sudden halt at the table.

Olivia let out a sigh of relief as the figure pulled up his black ninja hood, revealing the smiling face of Ivy's boyfriend, Brendan Daniels. No wonder he'd been superhumanly fast – he had been using his vamp super-speed!

Ivy wasn't smiling, though. 'What were you thinking?' she hissed to her boyfriend. 'I know it's Halloween and you're dressed like a ninja, but that doesn't mean you have to *act* like one. You can't let anyone see you using your powers!'

Brendan gave her a cheeky grin. 'I've got it covered, trust me. My cousin Maya's here, and she's dressed like a ninja, too. If any bunnies happen to see one of us cover too much ground too quickly, we can just explain it away by pointing out that there are two of us. Genius, huh?'

Ivy rolled her eyes even as she reached out to take his hand. 'Yes, fine, but you should still be *careful*.'

'Oof!' Brendan winced and pulled his hand free. 'You're giving me super-strong hand squeezes now? OK, you've made your point!' Laughing, he gave her a mock-salute. 'But right now, the Ninja of Doom has more people to scare and more justice to serve. *Beware the Ninja!*' Cackling, he pulled his hood up and dived back into the crowd.

Olivia tucked her hand into her sister's arm as Ivy watched him go, a mixture of affection and exasperation on her face.

'Some vamps do take advantage of Halloween,' Ivy said. 'I guess it's the one day of the year when we're not the strangest people in the room.'

Olivia grinned and nudged her. 'Come on, admit it. You totally thought that was cute.'

'I know!' Ivy groaned. 'It's terrible!' Shaking her head, she started walking again, arm-in-arm with Olivia. 'I just wish I didn't have vamp hearing tonight.'

'Why not?'

'Because I can hear greasy Josh and his band out in the hallway,' Ivy said glumly, 'and they're definitely plotting some kind of stunt. I just can't tell exactly what . . .'

A sudden wave of piercing cold swept through the room. Ivy stopped speaking and Olivia shuddered, wrapping her arms around herself. Goosebumps popped out all over her skin. Gasps and murmurs ran through the crowd.

Shivering, Olivia tucked herself closer to her sister . . . just as an eerie wind rushed over their heads, trailing a high, unearthly sound almost like a wail:

'*Aaahhhhhhh!*'

All the doors and windows of the café suddenly flew open with a bang, curtains billowing in the October chill.

Whoa. All the air seemed to suck itself out of the room, leaving Olivia breathless, as she waited with the rest of the guests for the big reveal.

What was about to step through those open doors? And how had Camilla managed that incredible effect?

But the doorway was completely empty . . . and a moment later, the doors and windows slammed shut again, all at once.

'Oooohhhhh!' The crowd let out a joint sigh of wonder . . . and fear.

Nervous giggles broke out along with gasps and excited chatter. But a moment later, applause rang through the room as the air suddenly turned warm again.

'Wow.' Even Olivia joined in the applause, clapping just as enthusiastically as her twin. 'Camilla really outdid herself with that one.'

Ivy nodded, beaming. 'The sound that that wind made was so *creepy*!'

'It actually wailed,' Olivia said. 'Just like . . .' Her hands shot up with surprise as she remembered: 'Just like that silly horoscope of Reiko's. Remember what it said? "The wailing winds of memory", or something like that.'

Ivy snorted. 'I'd already forgotten that silly thing.'

Olivia smiled at her twin's grumpy rejoinder, but inwardly, she wondered. *Did the horoscope* actually *predict our future?*

As the guests began to file out, Olivia went in hunt of Camilla, along with Ivy and Reiko, to give her the congratulations she deserved. When they found her, she was surrounded by a group of admirers, while Lillian smiled proudly in the background at her young protégé. Dressed as a Parisian film director, complete with clipboard and sunglasses, Camilla beamed at them all, her blonde curls springing out from underneath her beret.

'Did you really like it?'

'It was awesome!' Reiko said, bouncing on

65

her toes with excitement. 'The best Halloween party ever!'

'It really was amazing,' Olivia said. 'Especially that last effect, with the wind and the doors and windows. How did you pull *that* off?'

'A true artist never gives away her secrets, Olivia. Surely *you* know that!'

Olivia frowned at her friend – Camilla had half-turned when she spoke, as if she was addressing the guests filing out of Café Creative, rather than her.

Hmm. Olivia frowned. *Is Camilla hiding something?*

But it wasn't until the rest of the crowd had dispersed and the four girls were the only ones left in the café that Camilla's bright smile finally slipped. She turned back and fixed Olivia with a stare that was not freaked out as much as it was confused.

'What's wrong?' Olivia asked.

Moaning, Camilla slumped into an abandoned

chair and buried her face in her hands. 'That last effect totally freaked me out,' she groaned. 'Because the truth is, it had nothing to do with me!'

Olivia felt goosebumps rising along her arms. 'But if you didn't do it . . . who *did*?'

Chapter Four

O livia was still yawning as she left her house the next morning. Every time she'd fallen asleep last night, she'd been woken by memories of the spooky events at Café Creative. The strange girl in the red Victorian costume, the wind that had wailed through the room, slamming doors and giving everyone chills.

If the Halloween party's big finish hadn't been one of Camilla's planned effects, then who – or *what* – could have caused it?

When Camilla had admitted the truth, Olivia's first thought had been: *Ghost!*

It was the first thing she'd asked Ivy about

as they'd left the museum last night.

'Who knows if ghosts exist?' Ivy had shrugged, not looking nearly as freaked out as Olivia felt. 'Vampires have been debating for a long time whether there might be any other "paranormal" creatures. There have always been stories, but no proof. And besides . . .' She'd given Olivia a mischievous look, shadows falling over her face as they stepped outside. 'What we felt in there seemed more like a poltergeist to me!'

'A *what*?' Olivia had squeaked.

But their different family cars had been waiting for them, and she hadn't had time to get more out of her twin.

The moment she'd gotten home, though, she'd Googled the word "poltergeist" . . . and this morning, she was seriously regretting it! A ghost was alarming enough to think about, but an invisible ghost, intent on causing trouble, was a truly terrible thought!

No more late-night Internet searches for scary things, she ordered herself now, as she made her way up Undertaker Hill towards Ivy's house. She had made sure to get there earlier than usual.

Ivy wore a *serious* frown as she let Olivia inside. Glancing down the hallway, Olivia saw that, for the first time ever, the kitchen door was firmly shut.

'What's going on?' Olivia whispered. She couldn't stop staring at the closed kitchen door. Normally so inviting, it looked weirdly ominous now . . . especially since she could hear the faint sound of adult voices arguing behind it.

'Dad's convened a meeting,' Ivy said glumly. 'All the adult vamps in the neighbourhood were invited . . . but *only* the adults.' She sighed. 'Can you believe it? The whole community's on edge about what happened last night, like it was some really big deal. I'm almost sure – they think it *was* a ghost.'

'Whoa . . .' Olivia's eyes widened as she shut the

front door behind her. 'This is all very hard to get my head around.'

Ivy snorted, sweeping her long, dark hair back over her shoulder. 'Tell me about it!'

'Ahem.' The kitchen door opened, and their bio-dad stepped outside, giving them both a stern look.

Olivia winced. Even Ivy made a face.

'Whoops,' Ivy mumbled. 'I guess, of all people, I should really know better than to whisper about anybody in our family when they're within a mile of me!'

'*That* would be very sensible,' Charles said. 'But since you two are standing around talking about us . . .' Eyebrows raised, he waved them into the kitchen. 'You might as well join us.'

Trading an uncertain look, the twins followed after him.

There were four adults sitting at the table: Lillian, Albert from the museum, and Brendan's dad, Marc, and aunt, Carla. Their normally pale faces were all flushed, a sign of stress in vampires, and their red drinks all sat untouched in front of them.

Lillian gave the girls a quick, strained smile and patted the empty seats on either side of her. Olivia slid in gratefully beside her stepmother as Charles closed the kitchen door behind him.

'You're right,' he said to Ivy, 'this isn't the usual way we handle things here in Franklin Grove. But the truth is, we're all concerned. If what you've reported is true . . .'

'And it is,' Lillian cut in firmly. 'I was there, Charles. I saw and felt it all.'

Charles sighed. '. . . then that means that one of the vampire community's long-held and most-feared theories might be a reality.' He collapsed into a hard-backed chair, his usually straight shoulders slumping, as he finished: 'It's possible ghosts and spirits do exist!'

A chill seemed to fall over the whole room at his words. The other adults looked grimmer than ever.

Olivia looked from one vamp to another. No one spoke.

Olivia swallowed hard, seeing the strain on all the vamps' faces and feeling the urge to lighten the mood – somehow. Using all of her acting skills, she forced a grin. 'So,' she said. 'Does this mean I'm about to find out that Ivy and I have a secret ghost triplet?'

But not a single vampire laughed at her joke.

🦇   🦇   🦇

Ivy looked from one uber-serious face to the next. She rolled her eyes. 'Oh, come on!' she said. 'You guys all look like you've accidentally swallowed raw vegetables. Even if there *are* ghosts, what's the big deal? We're vampires, why should we be scared of them? Shouldn't we be, like, rejoicing? We might not be the Weirdest Weirdoes in Franklin Grove after all!'

'It's complicated,' Charles said heavily, as the other adults shifted in their seats. 'Of course, it's long been theorised that ghosts might exist, but no one has ever known for sure. Vampire research into spirits has been just as inconclusive as bunny research.'

'I know,' Ivy said impatiently, 'but I'm looking at a tableful of scaredy-bats, and I'm confused. If the worst a ghost can do is rattle a few windows and make it a bit draughty . . .' She shrugged. 'What do we have to worry about?'

Charles looked deadly serious. 'Humans,' he said. 'That's what we have to worry about.'

Across the table, Marc nodded. 'You must have noticed by now, Ivy,' he said. 'Any time something inexplicable happens, the bunny community starts asking questions.'

'Looking closer at things,' Carla added unhappily.

'And if *that* happens,' Charles finished for them,

'then our community will be at risk of exposure . . . which is why *we* have to get to the bottom of this before anyone else does!'

Ivy sighed. 'OK,' she admitted, 'that does make sense . . . except that no one except us even thinks it was a ghost. *Or* a poltergeist,' she added, and glimpsed Olivia's shudder in the corner of her eye.

Still, her twin backed her up. 'It's true,' Olivia said. 'They all assume that it was just a part of Camilla's show.'

'Ah, but you're forgetting one very important person.' Lillian grimaced. '*Camilla* knows it wasn't a part of the entertainment, and not only is she a smart girl, she's stubborn, too —when she puts on a show, she expects to be in charge of it! She'll think and think about what could have caused last night's incident until she drives herself crazy. Then she'll start investigating.'

'And once she does . . .' Charles shook his head, thin-lipped. 'As a whole, the vampire community does a good job of staying under the radar, but the fact is, we are living out in the open in Franklin Grove – more open than we were ever meant to be. The bunnies here have become accustomed to the fact that weird things happen in this town, but if they're ever given a reason to *think* about things . . .' He sighed. 'They'll realise that there was *always* something different about this place. And that will be the beginning of the end for us.'

Albert nodded vigorously. 'It's happened before, believe me! Why, I remember Prague, in 1908 . . .'

Uh-oh. Ivy propped her chin in her hand, sighing, as the old vampire got started. *I can tell this is the beginning of a very long story!*

Ivy wasn't wrong. Twenty minutes later, Albert was still talking. She fixed her dad with a pleading look. Obligingly, Charles gave a pointed cough, interrupting Albert mid-monologue. 'I'm afraid the girls are going to miss their bus if they don't hurry.'

Albert nodded wearily. 'Well, just don't forget what happened,' he said. 'I had to flee Prague in the middle of the night! I couldn't even bring along half of my painting supplies. And all because the locals realised I had violet eyes.' He sighed. 'Contact lenses were so hard to come by back then . . . and made of *glass*!'

'Ouch.' Olivia winced.

'But things have changed now!' Ivy rattled her fingers against the dining room table, almost desperate with impatience. 'We have real contact lenses, for one thing. We're not about to be chased out of town!'

'That's not actually what I'm worried about at the moment,' Charles said tensely. 'The truth is, I'm most worried about who will come *in* to Franklin Grove if word of this ghost gets out. If tourists start flooding in to investigate, the locals will have a very compelling reason to start looking closer. And if *that* happens . . .'

When Ivy boarded the school bus ten minutes later, her head was swimming with all the older vamps' dire warnings and with Albert's tale of woe. She slid into the seat behind Brendan, with Olivia close behind her . . . then let out a huff of frustration.

'What's up?' Brendan turned around, looping his arm over the top of the seat to grin down at her. 'C'mon, Vega. It's too early to be grumpy.'

'Not in our house.' Ivy tried to ignore the clawing sensation in her stomach, but at that very moment it gave a great grumble. 'Oh! I was so busy with the Conference of Doom, I completely forgot to grab any breakfast!' She slumped lower in her seat. 'Now I'm starving!'

'Here.' Brendan rummaged through his ragged black backpack and pulled out a snack-sized box of Marshmallow Platelets. 'It's not exactly a hearty meal, but at least it might keep you from getting too crabby. And that's good for all of us.' Winking, he passed the box to her.

'You're a life-saver!' Ivy ripped the box open.

'So how was the Conference of Doom?' asked Brendan curiously. 'My dad seemed pretty worried when he left for your house this morning.'

Ivy groaned and quickly filled him in on what had happened.

'This is the worst part of being a . . . being one of us,' she whispered to Brendan and Olivia once she'd finished. 'You know, if anyone else at school knew about vamps, they'd probably think it'd be super-cool to have our abilities and everything else – but that's because they don't know just how much *stress* it all comes with!' She shook her head in disbelief. 'We're only fourteen. Just think: when we're older, we're not only going to have all these same crazy worries, but we're going to be expected to, like, *do things* about them!'

Olivia grinned and gave her a nudge. 'Aren't you forgetting? Doing things about things is kind of our . . . *thing*!'

Despite herself, Ivy laughed. 'Good point, sis.'

Brendan reached over to cup his hand around her face, stroking her cheek gently with his thumb. 'How many mysteries have you solved so far, Ivy Holmes?'

'OK, OK.' Still laughing, Ivy scooped out a handful of Marshmallow Platelets and bit down happily. 'We'll do something about this one, too, if we can . . . just as soon as we think of a good way to approach it.'

Brendan shrugged, snagging a Marshmallow Platelet. His voice muffled, he said, 'You know, it felt more like a poltergeist than a ghost to me.'

'Aagh!' Olivia jumped up and grabbed him by the shoulders. 'Will everyone please stop saying that word? Otherwise *I'll* have to turn into a you-know-what and haunt you both!'

Ivy laughed so hard that she accidentally spat out her Marshmallow Platelets. 'Look out,' she finally gasped to Brendan. 'Or it'll be the Mystery of the Perky Pink Poltergeist next!'

Olivia cringed. 'What did I *just* say?'

After school Olivia followed her sister down the street towards the Franklin Grove Museum.

'We need to start at the beginning,' Ivy was saying. 'Whether it was an actual ghost, or there's some rational explanation, I'm sure that we'll find a real clue at Café Creative!'

'A clue, hmm?' Olivia gave her a gently chiding look. 'You do remember you're not wearing the deerstalker any more, right?'

'I know. Don't you miss it?' Ivy heaved a mock sigh as she pushed open the big front door of the museum. 'I kind of liked that hat, actually. Now if only I could find a black one, with bat-shaped ear flaps. I could be Goth Holmes! The latest style!'

Olivia closed her lips firmly, but she couldn't completely hold back a giggle as she imagined it. 'Now that's an image that deserves to go viral on the Vorld Vide Veb!'

'Better than the Happy Vampire, that's for sure.' Ivy scowled.

'I dunno . . . she was kind of cute,' Olivia said, batting her eyelashes. Then she took off running before her vamp twin could grab her.

She skidded to a halt in the doorway of Café Creative. *Hmm . . . it's going to be hard to do any investigating here!*

Under Lillian's management, the café had become a huge success. Today customers were filling almost all of the tables, sipping frothy coffee drinks and smoothies, while other visitors wandered through the open space around them, picking up the pens, felt tips and paint brushes that had been left out for community use and making their own contribution to the latest mural growing on the walls.

Unfortunately, now that the café was so popular, it was a lot harder for the twins to snoop around with any subtlety.

As Olivia and Ivy peered into corners and knocked on walls looking for hidden compartments, Olivia caught more than one visitor giving them strange looks. And when Ivy started poking around underneath the tables, Olivia winced at the expression on the faces of the customers who sat there. They pulled in their legs and tugged their bags closer.

'Um . . . Ivy?' Olivia beckoned to her twin as Ivy emerged from one table and started towards the next. 'Do we even know what we're really looking for?' she whispered.

Ivy's shoulders sagged. 'Not really,' she confessed. 'Just . . . anything weird. Right?'

Before Olivia could answer, a rasping voice sounded just behind them.

'You two!' It was Joan Calhoun, the head barista.

She glared at them, her muscled arms crossed over her apron. 'You girls may be related to my manager, but that doesn't mean you're allowed to loiter around here and disturb my customers. If you're not going to order food, or' – she jerked her chin meaningfully at the community mural on the walls – '*doodle* something, then you need to find somewhere else to be. Got it?'

'Sorry.' Olivia cringed. As her twin mumbled an apology of her own, Olivia took a deep breath and turned on actor-mode. 'Actually . . .' Smiling ruefully, she sidled up to the café counter. 'Could I order a cake and orange juice, please? That was why we came here in the first place. We were just distracted by . . . erm . . . remembering how amazing the Halloween party was.'

'That's right,' Ivy agreed, nodding vigorously. 'We were . . . uh . . . looking for *clues* to how Camilla did the special effects.'

'Hmmph.' Joan grimaced as she stepped behind

the counter and pulled out a bottle of orange juice from the refrigerated case. 'I'm just glad I wasn't working that night. Unlike some people, I don't find scares fun.'

Olivia gave a heartfelt sigh of agreement. 'You and me both!'

'Besides . . .' Joan shook her head as she uncapped the orange juice. 'Living in Franklin Grove my whole life, I've had more than enough of the real thing to deal with.'

Uh-oh. Olivia felt Ivy tense beside her. It took all of her acting training to keep a sympathetic smile on her own face as she said, 'What do you mean?'

Please, please, please don't let those scares have been vamp-related!

'Haven't you ever heard the legends?' Joan fixed her with a beady look. 'This town is full of spectres!'

Olivia's eyes widened. 'You mean . . . ghosts?'

'Oh, yes.' Joan didn't even bother to look down

at the orange juice she was pouring. Her gaze held Olivia's with magnetic intensity. 'Most people around here seem to have forgotten the old stories, but not us Calhouns. According to my grandma, back down South, our family used to be a wealthy lot. We moved up here in the late nineteenth century, and we have a legend of our own.' She leaned across the counter, lowering her voice to a very serious whisper. 'Apparently – and you two will appreciate this part – there were a pair of twin sisters, my great-great-great aunts, who were separated by tragedy in their teenage years. We have a portrait of them right here in this museum, you know.'

'Twin sisters!' Olivia breathed, leaning closer. 'I saw that portrait.'

'It's a good one, isn't it?' Joan nodded. 'But it's not a happy story. According to old family lore, the tragedy that separated the twins left their souls restless in the afterlife. Now, one of the sisters is said to be forever trapped here, cursed to haunt our town – and you can tell when you've seen her, because she's always decked out in a fancy red dress.'

A red dress . . .?

Olivia used every ounce of her acting ability to keep her voice from quivering. 'What were their names?' she asked Joan.

But she had a horrible feeling that she already knew half of the answer.

🦇　　　🦇　　　🦇

Five minutes later, Olivia's legs gave out in the museum hallway as she stared once again at the portrait of the Victorian twin sisters: Patience and Hope Calhoun. She leaned back against the wall and slid helplessly to the ground, her gaze still fixed on their faces . . .

Their *familiar* faces.

'I can't believe it . . . I might actually have talked to a ghost!' she whispered. 'It would explain why the girl in that fabulous red dress was behaving so strangely at Camilla's party. I thought she was just in costume . . .' She shook her head helplessly. 'Could I really have been talking to the ghost of Patience Calhoun?'

'Hey, woah there,' said Ivy, sliding down beside her. 'Remember, we still don't know any of this for sure. Until we do, there's no point overthinking it.'

'You're right,' Olivia said. 'But, still . . . Joan's story is kind of checking out.'

'I know, but we still need proof. Until we have some, we should keep an eye out for that girl you were talking to.'

'You're right,' Olivia said firmly. 'There could be a perfectly rational explanation . . . and if there is, we'll find it. But . . . what now?'

Ivy sighed, thunking her head back against the wall. 'I have to admit, I was just wondering the same thing!' Her eyes narrowed. 'But actually . . . maybe I *do* have an idea. Why don't we go see

Camilla and get the full details of exactly what she *was* planning for the party? Who knows, maybe there was some kind of technical malfunction. She was using a lot of fancy equipment – for all we know, something could have gone wrong, and *that's* what really caused all the spooktacular stuff. All this fuss could be for nothing!'

'You might be right,' Olivia said, as she took out her phone to call her friend.

❤   ❤   ❤

Olivia had been in Camilla's room countless times since she'd first moved to Franklin Grove. But she'd never seen it look like this. Camilla's mother had let the twins into the house and sent them upstairs, and when Olivia first opened the bedroom door, she couldn't even see her friend inside beneath all the chaos.

It looks like Lillian was right – Camilla may just have gone crazy!

Two huge new corkboards had been hung on

opposite walls of the bedroom, each of them completely covered in masses of newspaper clippings, photos, and random scraps of paper with notes scrawled all over them. Long lines of coloured string ran between the two corkboards, forming a spiderweb of connections across the room, with sticky notes attached to each string.

'Come on in!' Camilla's voice sounded from across the room. She was kneeling underneath the final lengths of string, scribbling notes. She looked up with a mad glint in her eyes. 'But don't disturb anything!'

'Um . . . OK.' Olivia shot a wide-eyed look at Ivy before crouching down in front of the tangle of string that filled the room. She kept her questions to herself as she carefully crawled underneath the tendrils, but as soon as she reached her friend, she gently laid a hand on Camilla's shoulder. 'Can you tell us what's going on here?'

'I can't stop thinking about what happened on

Halloween!' Camilla raked her hand through her spiralling curls, rattling out her words with just as much intensity as if she were in the middle of shooting one of her movies. 'It was just too weird! My parents told me to stop worrying about it, but I can't, because something was *very* wrong! And at first I thought I was overreacting, imagining that it had to be something unnatural – but the more I look into things, the less crazy I think I am. *You* don't think I'm crazy, do you?'

'Uh . . .' Olivia looked helplessly at her sister, who was crouching behind her.

Before either of them could answer, Camilla raced on, wildly jabbing her fingers towards the corkboards. 'I had no idea until I started researching,' she babbled, 'but this Halloween was *not* the first time there've been reports of a poltergeist in Franklin Grove.'

Olivia winced. 'Could we *please* use another word for it?' she begged.

Camilla shrugged impatiently. 'Whatever you want to call it, this town is full of ghost-like phenomena. Look!' She pushed past Olivia and Ivy to wriggle out from under the mass of strings. As soon as she was free, she started jabbing at different notes on the boards. 'See all these different incidents? They're all reports of doors slamming shut or swinging open, windowpanes rattling, and eerie, howling winds. And it's always around this time of year!'

Ivy gave a nervous-sounding laugh as she followed Camilla out from under the strings. 'Well . . . at least the howling wind has an obvious explanation. The wind always gets a little more "howly" in the autumn, doesn't it?'

'That's true.' Olivia crawled after her twin. 'In fact, in Franklin Grove, we could probably rename the whole holiday "Howl-oween"!'

Camilla shook her head irritably, picking her way through the strings until she found the one she wanted. 'As soon as I figured out those details, I started digging, tracing all these incidents back as far as possible. Apparently, this kind of stuff didn't start getting reported until the 1860s. So I decided to research some local history, see if there were any significant historical events in Franklin Grove that happened at the end of October in the 1860s. And guess what?' She pinched the yellow string she'd found, holding it up as she followed it to the corkboard on the opposite wall. 'I found one story that fits *perfectly*.' With a grin of fierce concentration, she pointed to the note that was attached to the yellow string. 'That wind that we heard sounded anguished, didn't it? Like the howl of a person in pain.'

'Well . . .' Olivia shifted uncomfortably. *Don't panic,* she told herself. *Remember what Ivy said.* 'It did kind of *sound* like someone in distress,' she admitted, 'but I'm sure there must be some rational explanation . . .'

'Oh, there is.' Camilla pointed to the corkboard, where a photo of a much-too-familiar portrait had been stuck. 'And I've found it! See, there was one girl in the 1860s who had *more* than enough to be distressed about, and her name was Patience Calhoun . . .'

Chapter Five

I vy was wearing her best stomping boots as she, Olivia, Sophia and Reiko all headed towards the Meat and Greet diner for breakfast the next morning. Even her vamptastic bat-patterned black leather footwear wasn't enough to cheer her up, though . . . not when the adult vamps were acting more freaked out than ever.

The girls might have nosed out a good lead the day before, but the mystery was still unsolved; and worse, Camilla had posted a blog, asking if anyone in Franklin Grove knew of any "spooky legends" – she was pretending she was researching for a new movie idea, but it was obvious what her real motive was – and that it was exactly the kind of thing that was going to put the vamp community on edge. That morning, Ivy's dad had been practically vibrating with tension as he'd eaten his breakfast. Every time he'd tried to hold a piece of silverware, it had rattled against his plate like the worst drum solo ever. But when the rest of the girls had come by to pick Ivy up, he'd leaped up like a black-clad jack-in-the-box and given them all strict orders to Act Normal!

Which was kind of a joke, coming from him, Ivy thought glumly as she strode down the street.

The adult vamps were determined not to let anything seem odd or even slightly "off" to anyone in town, not when their own secret hung by such a fragile thread. And unfortunately, Ivy wasn't sure any more that they were wrong about that. She'd spent half the night tossing and turning, worrying about what would happen if the bunnies of Franklin Grove really did figure out the truth.

Of course, that meant she had spent the other half of the night nursing her new bruises! *Ow.* She rubbed her shoulder where she'd hit it hard against her coffin as she'd tossed and turned. *A coffin is not a safe place for a stressed-out vampire.* She'd finally given up and climbed out, turning on her computer to read up on the Calhoun twins, but there hadn't been much to find.

Where on earth had Camilla *got* all of that information? *The girl really must be obsessed!*

Ivy frowned as she looked down the street and glimpsed a familiar dark-haired figure in a leather jacket and jeans lunging out of the front door of the Meat and Greet as if he were fleeing a stake-wielding mob. 'Where's Brendan going? He was supposed to meet us there.'

Even as she spoke, her boyfriend turned and saw them. Waving his arms, he rushed up the street. His gorgeous dark hair was mussed up and his leather jacket sat crookedly on his shoulders, as if he'd pulled it on in a hurry.

'What's up?' Ivy asked him.

'Let's just say . . .' Brendan slid a panicked look back towards the Meat and Greet. 'I think we'd better find somewhere else for breakfast.'

'How come?' Ivy frowned. 'We always eat there. And we're supposed to be acting "normal".'

'Yeah, but . . .' Grimacing, Brendan ran a hand through his hair, messing it up even more. 'Look, the *diner's* not acting normal, OK? And besides, it's kind of . . . full.'

'Seriously?' Ivy glanced down at her watch. 'How could it possibly be full this early on Saturday morning?'

Sophia, looking stylish as always in a fitted black coat and high-heeled black boots, leaned in. 'What's going on, Brendan?'

Brendan sighed. 'I guess you might as well all come and see for yourselves.'

Ivy started for the diner with a scowl on her

face. Every vamp-sense she had was tingling with the certainty that there was danger ahead.

Even before they stepped inside, she could see for herself that it was packed. People lined the tables against the front windows. When Ivy peered through the glass front door, she could see that the crowd was two deep at the counter.

'Is there some kind of event going on that we didn't hear about?' Olivia asked.

'It doesn't look that organised,' Ivy said grimly, 'but it sure does look like everyone's excited about *something*.'

Everywhere she looked, she could see animated conversations going on, with people leaning across the tables, hands waving. The glass was too thick for her to make out any words, but the buzz of tension and excitement inside was so strong, she could practically feel it.

Then her eye fell on Josh Dillon and his greasy cronies, all clumped together at a corner table.

Uh-oh.

'Come on,' she said firmly. 'It's time to get inside and do some eavesdropping.'

Brendan grimaced. 'OK,' he said, 'but brace yourself.'

Ivy opened the door . . . and fell back a step, staggering as a wall of pure noise hit her sensitive vampire ears. *Ouch!*

Gritting her teeth, she stepped into the crowded diner. She forced herself to breathe deeply to steady herself as she waited for her hearing to adjust to the painful intensity of the noise. Gradually, she began to pick out individual words . . . or rather, the same words, over and over again.

'. . . ghosts . . .'

'. . . spirits . . .'

'. . . *woooooohh*!'

Ivy's shoulders relaxed as she looked around. No one had made the leap to vampires yet, thank darkness. But . . . She frowned as her gaze passed over all the unfamiliar faces in the diner.

'I've never seen most of these people before,' she said.

'That's because they're from out of town,' Brendan replied unhappily.

'I guess the news must have spread,' Sophia agreed, looking around the room.

Ivy exchanged a worried look with the other vampires.

There were fresh eyes in town. And that meant a whole lot more people about to notice any vampire behaving suspiciously.

How did Camilla's blog post spread so fast? We'll have to be so careful.

Behind Ivy, Olivia heaved a sigh. 'I just don't understand,' she said. 'Why would the rumour of ghosts bring strangers *to* Franklin Grove? Wouldn't that keep most people *away*?'

'Are you joking?' Reiko stared at her. 'I would *love* to meet a ghost. I'd have so many questions . . .'

Ivy let the rest of her friend's words drift into the background as she moved slowly along the line of tables, straining to pick up on the one conversation that worried her the most. She kept her eyes on the clock on the far wall, squinting as if she were trying to make out the time, but all of her attention was on the table in the corner where Josh sat with his gang.

Josh looking that excited can't be a good sign!

It was hard to pick up individual voices in the mass of sound that pressed at her from all directions, but finally, she made out Josh's smug voice. 'He replied to my email *himself*, you know, and he says he's *definitely* thinking about coming here to check out the town!'

Oh, this does not sound good at all. Swallowing hard, Ivy drifted closer, keeping her head carefully tilted away from them.

She had to find out more, no matter how little she liked it . . .

And she liked it even less when she realised exactly who the greasy gang was talking about.

'I can't believe it,' Ivy said miserably, five minutes later.

They'd had to leave the Meat and Greet when they finally ran out of excuses to loiter in the aisles. Olivia had even tried to book a table so that they could stand and wait for it, but the man behind the counter had told them they might have to wait until Sunday night for that. Now they sat on a bench near the diner, huddled together in the cold air for a whispered meeting.

Ivy groaned as she looked down at Brendan's phone. Brendan was busily tapping at the keypad, looking up a clip of *Gregor Gleka, Ghost Grabber!*

'I've heard of him,' Brendan said. 'He's got a weekly cable TV show, doesn't he?'

'I know.' Ivy slumped as he pulled up several pages' worth of video results online, each of them with hundreds of thousands of views. 'Lillian and

I watched an episode once – there was nothing else on TV and we were super bored. It was one of the most ridiculous, trashiest shows I've ever had to sit through!'

'Wow.' Olivia shot her a mischievous look. 'That's really saying something, coming from a fan of *Shadowtown*!'

'Ooohhh.' Brendan made a mock-offended face even as he pressed "play" on the first YouTube clip. 'Them's fighting words!'

But Ivy was too worried to even consider a death-squint in defence of her favourite guilty pleasure.

Watching a stupid show on TV was one thing . . . but having that show actually *take over her town*?

'I don't understand.' Reiko frowned down at the tiny image of Gregor Gleka on-screen, wearing a flashy black-and-crimson shirt with sleeves that billowed around him when he gestured. 'What is this?'

Ivy scowled. 'It's a so-called "paranormal investigation" show.' She made air-quotes around the words, her tone dripping with contempt. 'A camera follows Gregor around while he "investigates" incidents involving the paranormal and supernatural.'

'He links all the "unexplained events" he investigates to old myths and legends from other places,' Sophia said. "He's always going on and on about the stories he's heard "back home". Isn't he from somewhere in Eastern Europe?'

'So he claims,' Ivy muttered. 'But to *me*, his accent is less "I grew up in Eastern Europe," and more "I backpacked around Europe one summer and now I'm faking it."'

Olivia frowned down at Brendan's phone as the clip continued. 'I don't like the way he talks to people.'

As they watched, Gregor hounded civilian after civilian in whatever town he was visiting, throwing aggressive, leading questions at them.

'You say the glass *levitated*?'

Each time, the response from the interviewee was the same. A slight cringe, and a reluctant nod. 'It, you know, it kind of . . . *wobbled*. It looked weird, but maybe there's . . .'

The interviewee would never get to finish their thought. At the first sign of disagreement, Gregor would pivot away, taking his microphone with him, flashing his trademark expression of intense concentration – his white teeth glinting and his dark eyes widening until he looked almost manic. 'Undeniable proof of ghostly activity! At last, the truth is out!' he declared. 'My mission continues, for I will never rest – not until the spirits do.'

'Ooohhh.' Reiko's eyes widened as she watched. 'Good line.'

'Huh.' Ivy shrugged irritably. 'I don't know. I can't tell if it's just dumb, or if it's so cheesy it's actually brilliant. All I know is, the *last* thing we need right now is for Gleka to get hundreds of thousands of people thinking that something paranormal is going on in Franklin Grove. So . . .' She tapped Brendan's phone to halt playback and looked from one of her friends to another, thinking hard. 'We're going to have to throw Josh's gang off the scent, and fast, if we want to keep Gregor away . . .'

She looked to her twin.

'. . . and that's going to take some serious acting skills.'

🦇   🦇   🦇

Every so often, Olivia really wished that she hadn't stumbled into an acting career. Oh, sure, there were upsides – movie sets, international travel, meeting the boy of her dreams – but there were also serious downsides, like mean girls on message boards who hated her for being with Jackson . . . and moments when her own friends nominated her to do some on-the-spot "acting" to get them out of trouble.

At least this performance, unlike her upcoming film scenes, wouldn't require a Southern accent. This time she was playing a simple role: *Olivia Abbott, chatterbox.*

'Oh, it was amaaaazing!' she squealed into her cell phone, four feet away from Josh and the greasy gang's table in the Meat and Greet. She was fake-wandering down the aisle just a few inches at a time, as if she were so wrapped up in her conversation that she didn't even realise that anyone else could hear her . . . especially the boys whose table she was secretly aiming for. 'I just soooo wish you could have been at Café Creative for the party, Jackson,' she said loudly. She had to hide a wince at the rolled eyes of the customers at the nearby table, whose conversations were being interrupted by her blasting voice.

Remember: this is what we want! For the sake of every vamp in town, she needed as many people as possible to overhear her. So she added a happy little bounce to her next step, and pretended not to notice the annoyed huff of the man whose foot she'd just trodden on.

'Camilla put together the most incredible, spooky effects for Halloween! *Especially* the last one,' she added, as she drifted to a halt by the boys' table. 'I could hardly believe how real it felt. She actually rigged all the doors and windows to open on a timer at the end of the show. Everyone *totally* freaked out!'

Tipping her head to one side, she paused and faked a look of concentration, as if she were listening to "Jackson" on the other end of the phone . . . which she had actually turned off. Then she plastered a huge smile on her face, as if Jackson had just said something wonderful.

'I know! It was the *best* idea of yours to call in a favour with our director. That machinery he loaned Camilla for the party was unbelievable. Honestly, if I hadn't known better, I'd have been fooled into thinking there was a real ghost, too!'

There. Still beaming, Olivia slipped a glance at the table next to her . . . and the smile slipped right off her face.

All five boys were hunched over games on their phones, their eyes fixed to the screens, their thumbs darting madly over the keys.

'C'mon, c'mon . . . yes!' Josh pumped his fist in the air. 'I *rock*, losers!'

They didn't hear a word I said.

Not a single person at any of the tables was paying attention to Olivia's too-loud phone call. They'd all shut it out to focus on their own conversations, leaning towards each other and gesturing intensely.

Crud. This isn't working. Apparently, not even mentioning Hollywood contacts was enough to distract ghost-hunters from their wild theories!

So much for that plan. 'Goodbye, Jackson,' Olivia mumbled. She slipped the cell phone back into her purse as she walked out of the Meat and Greet, her steps dragging.

Obviously, they were going to need to try even harder. Which meant it might just be time to bring in an *actual* Hollywood contact . . .

🦇　　　🦇　　　🦇

Twenty minutes later, still upset by Olivia's failure, Ivy and the others streamed into Café Creative for a second attempt at breakfast and another desperate brainstorming session. The café was nearly as packed as the Meat and Greet today, but Ivy was relieved to see that it wasn't full of ghost-hunting conspiracy buffs. *Maybe the creative atmosphere repelled them,* she thought. *Or maybe even the ghost-hunters don't want to be in a room that might* actually *be haunted!*

The café was full of busy groups working quietly on artistic projects, from friends scribbling in notebooks side-by-side, to sketch-artists and mural-painters. It was just the kind of vibe that Lillian had envisioned for this space . . .

. . . although Ivy was pretty sure that any health inspectors would *not* be impressed by the fact that Albert was painting a watercolour only inches from his meal. Although she didn't envy any uppity inspectors who tried to criticise the cranky old vampire – personally, she wouldn't dare!

Joan harrumphed as they approached her counter. 'I hope you're planning to actually stay and eat the food you order this time!'

Ivy saw her twin cringe at the reminder of the way they'd abandoned the café other day. 'Sorry. I just . . . um . . .'

'This time, we're staying,' Ivy assured the glowering barista. 'Don't worry. We're starving! And today, I *really* need my coffee.'

While Joan pulled their pastries out from the glass display case, Reiko bounced on her toes and scanned the café as if looking for a tennis opponent she was determined to beat. 'Right. Where are we going to sit?'

Olivia frowned as she picked up her croissant and her smoothie. 'If we want to be able to talk in private, maybe . . . over there?' She pointed at the far side of the room, where there were three empty tables in a row.

'I might have a better idea,' Ivy said reluctantly, bracing herself. *Ivy Holmes must show no fear!* 'We should ask someone who *really* knows what's been going on here . . . forever!'

The other girls sighed as she pointed at Albert, but none of them argued. The museum's caretaker might be grumpy, but he was also the best source of information in the café, and maybe in all of Franklin Grove.

Now Ivy just had to figure out how to get him started on exactly the right old story. *At least it's good training for becoming an investigative journalist*, she told herself.

But when she turned around, she found Olivia already standing next to the vampire caretaker, staring open-mouthed at his watercolour painting.

'That's the red dress . . .' Olivia breathed. 'That's the girl who was sitting at my table on Halloween!'

Ivy looked over Olivia's shoulder to see that Albert's painting was of a girl with pinned curls, wearing a red dress exactly like the one Olivia had described on the girl she had met at the party.

Albert's brush stopped moving. He let out a heavy sigh. Then he looked up at Ivy's twin, his expression pained. 'You saw her?' he asked. 'If you did, I believe I can guess exactly what she said to you that night. She asked if you had seen her sister, didn't she?'

Olivia nodded, gulping.

Jackpot! This was exactly the kind of information they needed. Ivy and the others all huddled around him to take in every word.

'What can you tell us about her?' Ivy demanded.

For the first time that she could remember, she saw a smile on Albert's face, though it was tinged with sadness. He carefully wiped off his paintbrush. 'That's a long story, I'm afraid. But it all began over a century ago, when I first met a girl named Patience Calhoun.' He nodded meaningfully at the dark-haired girl in his painting, lowering his voice to a whisper.

'I've been keeping this to myself for far too long. I didn't even mention it to the others at the meeting because – well, I couldn't bear to bring it up. But since it sounds like . . .' Ivy saw disbelief in the old vampire's eyes, just for a moment. Then he nodded, as if making a decision. '. . . yes, since Olivia might actually have met Patience herself . . .'

He picked up his cup of tea, but he didn't take a sip, his expression weary as he cradled the full cup in both hands. 'The girls' father, Cornelius Calhoun, was a wealthy merchant from the South. He often travelled for business, and would take Patience and Hope with him to broaden their horizons. They must have moved up here when they were about your age. One autumn, Cornelius's business took him all the way across the ocean to England. The girls were both terribly excited about the sights they would see there. Unfortunately, when the time came for their departure, Mrs Calhoun was too sick to travel. She couldn't stay at home by herself, so one of the twins had to stay behind and look after their mother. After a great deal of discussion, it was decided that Patience would stay, and Hope would go with Cornelius.'

Oh, ouch. Ivy had already heard the basics of this story from Camilla, but hearing the details now, in Albert's trembling whisper, felt so much worse. 'They never came back, did they?' she said quietly.

'Never.' Albert's lips compressed into a thin line for a moment before he managed to continue. 'In those days, of course, the journey was by ship, not by plane, and the sea was occasionally . . . unkind.' His face tightened again and he lifted one hand to brush quickly at his left eye, which seemed to be sparkling oddly.

Is he actually crying? Ivy would never have imagined it of the crotchety old vampire. 'How well did you know the girls?' she asked, her voice softening.

'Better than anyone realised,' he replied. 'I was a youngster myself when this tragedy happened, and we kept our friendship secret.'

'Ahhh,' Sophia said knowingly. 'The rich girls' parents didn't want them mixing with an ordinary boy?'

'That wasn't it at all.' Albert's shoulders rose and fell in a sigh. 'No, by my family's particular standards, the Calhoun twins were far more ordinary than us, simply because they were human. It was *my* parents who discouraged me from getting too close to either of them, for fear of putting our secret at risk. They didn't understand . . .' He broke off, shaking his head.

117

Ivy felt a twist of sympathy. Her own bunny twin was already reaching out to take Albert's hand, and – astonishingly – Albert didn't pull it away.

Ivy tried to make her voice gentle as she asked the question she couldn't avoid: 'Do you really think Patience's ghost is haunting Franklin Grove? Camilla's done some research, and there's a pattern of strange things happening at Halloween. And now with what went on at the party . . .'

Albert nodded. 'Clearly, your sister met Patience – she never got over losing her twin. Her spirit must ache with the loss . . .'

Instinctively, Ivy looked to her own twin. Olivia was still clasping Albert's hand in both of hers, but she was gazing at Ivy, her face stricken.

How would either of them keep going if they lost each other? Ivy couldn't bear to imagine it.

Gradually, though, the sound of Albert's voice trickled back into her awareness.

'. . . and as for the timing, Hope was supposed to

return home at the end of October that year. The girls planned to celebrate their delayed fourteenth birthday party on the day of Halloween itself. It was their tradition that they always took tea in the grounds of their house together on their birthday, just the two of them. Patience had already chosen Hope's birthday present, months ahead of time. She couldn't wait to give it to her. But of course Hope never arrived for her birthday tea that year – and Patience never celebrated another birthday again.'

Chapter Six

'I'm sorry,' Olivia said, as her vamp friends took in Albert's story. 'I really have to go. *Now.*' She turned and hurried away from the table, leaving the vampires to debate their theories. She felt terrible for leaving, but her thoughts were making her heart heavy.

How would I feel if Ivy went away, but never came home?

Taking a deep breath, Olivia stepped back into the long, echoing hallway that led out of the museum. She pulled out her cell phone and hit the button to call Camilla. *There. Keeping an eye on my best friend for the vamps' sake has to be a lot less sad than going ghost-hunting with Ivy and the others! Maybe I can talk*

Camilla into just watching old romantic comedies with me for a while.

When Camilla answered her phone, though, she sounded out of breath, and the sounds of honking car horns blared in the background. 'Olivia! I was just heading out.'

So much for a quiet movie afternoon. Olivia frowned as she stepped through the museum's big front door, blinking against the bright autumn sunlight. 'Where are you going?'

'The park,' Camilla said.

Whew. Olivia's shoulders relaxed. *That sounds safe.* 'Are you filming something new there?' she asked brightly.

'Nope. I'm *investigating.*' Camilla lowered her voice to an intense whisper. 'Believe it or not, our local park is exactly where the old Calhoun house was once located!'

Oh, no. More ghost-hunting! Olivia bit back a sigh, her steps slowing down. 'Camilla, it's just a park.

The house isn't even there any more. What exactly do you think you're going to find?'

'I have no idea! But I have a really strong feeling.' Camilla let out a muffled grunt of frustration. 'I know it sounds crazy. But, who knows? Maybe when I'm actually standing on the grounds where Patience Calhoun once lived, I'll *experience* something.'

Uh-oh. The last thing any of the Franklin Grove vamps needed was for Camilla to have a face-to-face meeting with a ghost – especially if she was armed with a camera. 'I really think . . .' Olivia began.

'Sorry, I've gotta go. I'll let you know later how it went!' The phone clicked off as Camilla hung up.

Drat. Stomping her foot, Olivia typed in a quick, warning text message to Ivy. Then she started to run, cursing her beloved kitten-heeled ankle boots.

She had to head Camilla off before her friend could get to know Patience Calhoun any better!

🦇　　　🦇　　　🦇

Olivia caught up with Camilla just before both girls reached the front gate of the park, running from opposite directions.

'Whew!' Olivia grabbed hold of the gate's iron bars and lifted one aching foot to ease the burn. 'I'm so glad I found you.'

'You came!' Camilla flopped against the other side of the gate, panting. 'I couldn't . . . wait to get here . . . and get started. But . . .' She beamed at Olivia as she straightened. 'I'm so glad you decided to join me! Thank you for not thinking I'm crazy!'

'Trust me.' Breathing hard, Olivia set her sore foot back on the ground. *Next time, I'm definitely putting on running shoes before any high-speed chases!* Still, she managed to summon up a weak smile for her best friend. 'I might be sceptical about ghosts, but I would never think you're crazy.'

'Well, you might be the only one who doesn't.' Camilla shrugged philosophically. 'It comes with the territory. When you've got a good imagination, people tend not to take you seriously.'

'*I* do.' Olivia squeezed her friend's arm. 'I just have to ask, though . . . is there any way I can talk you out of this? Because I'd *so* much rather take you over to Mister Smoothie to hang out and talk about something else . . . or head back to your house to watch rom-coms all afternoon.'

For a moment, Camilla looked wistful. Then she lifted her chin, her expression turning stern. 'I can't,' she said. 'I'm sorry, but I really will go crazy if I don't find out everything I can.'

'OK.' Olivia sighed. She knew her friend well enough to realise there was no point arguing with her any more. 'In that case, I'll come with you.'

Camilla flashed her a smile. 'You're the best.'

Olivia's return smile felt more than a little strained. *This doesn't count as lying . . . does it?* She really did want to support her friend. But for the sake of every vamp in town she *also* wanted to make sure that Camilla didn't find out too much.

Camilla pulled out her phone as she stepped through the gate. Her eyes darted around the wide field, which was still covered in a thin layer of dew that sparkled in the sunlight. 'OK, I've downloaded an old map from the Internet, so we should be able to locate the site where the Calhoun house once stood. This way!'

She pointed ahead, and the girls followed the map past the skateboard ramps and the picnic tables, towards the wooded area on the Lincoln Vale side of the park. The air was crisp and cold, but the sun was bright. Olivia spotted kids from her school doing tricks on the ramps, while young children and their parents, bundled up in layers, filled the playground area. It was easy to forget, as they walked across the park, that they weren't just enjoying the fresh air on a pretty November day . . .

. . . until Olivia glimpsed a girl in a red, Victorian-style dress in the trees just ahead of them.

Oh, no! Her heart-rate suddenly doubled. But by the time she'd blinked and looked again, the flash of bright colour was gone.

'Did you see that?' Camilla was breathing in quick pants as she hurried into the woods. 'I can't believe it!'

'I . . . didn't see anything,' Olivia lied. She grabbed Camilla's arm. 'Maybe we should –'

'I have to get closer!' Camilla pulled free and crept forwards between the trees, her footsteps crunching against fallen twigs and old leaves.

'I really don't think this is a good idea!' Olivia said. 'And besides, wait! . . . I think we misread the map. Look, the house is back that way!' She pointed towards the playground, far behind them.

'Maybe so,' Camilla whispered, 'but that flash I saw was up ahead.'

'Camilla, please! I just . . . I have a really bad feeling about this. *Please* come back.'

Camilla stopped, resting one hand on the closest tree as she lowered her head for a moment. When she turned back to look at Olivia, her face was full of regret. 'I'm sorry,' she said. 'But I can't stop now. I've got to figure out the truth!'

'But . . .' Olivia began.

It was too late. Camilla was already hurrying deeper into the woods, leaving Olivia behind.

This would be so much easier if Ivy and the others were here! Olivia looked over her shoulder, through the first few rows of trees to the park beyond, but there was no sign of her sister or any of their friends. Either Ivy hadn't gotten her text message, or she was confident that Olivia could handle this by herself.

Olivia wasn't so sure about that. But Camilla was already hidden in the dense forest ahead, and she couldn't let her best friend run into trouble on her own.

Biting her lip to hold back a whimper, she

followed, catching up just as Camilla let out a gasp.

'There!'

The back of a red hoop skirt vanished behind a tree far ahead.

'Come on!' Camilla hissed. 'But don't let it see us!'

Together, the two girls raced from tree to tree, staying covered, as they followed the girl in the Victorian dress. She was moving fast, lunging between tree trunks, and Olivia only caught occasional glimpses of her speeding through the trees, carrying an elegant white parasol over her head. Camilla had whipped out her cell phone and was trying to aim its camera at the figure.

'Why,' Olivia panted, 'is she running so fast?'

'Who knows?' Camilla's voice was shaking with exhilaration. 'But I can't wait to find out! I wish I'd brought a better camera. Just think: in a couple of minutes, I might be interviewing a real ghost!'

That would be a disaster! Olivia thought. But she

had to focus on her running now, so she wouldn't slam into any branches on the way.

Finally, the girl ahead of them came to a stop.

Holding her breath, Olivia crept forwards, moving her boots as gently as she could through the twig- and leaf-covered grass. At her side, Camilla's face was bright pink, and her hands shook as she raised her cell phone, camera at the ready.

Olivia took a deep breath. *OK, this is it. Am I ready for another ghost encounter?*

Maybe if she offered to hold Camilla's camera for the interview, she could accidentally "forget" to turn it on, and then . . .

The ghost girl kicked the tree in front of her, hard.

Whoa. Olivia's eyebrows flew up as she saw the tree shudder under the blow. *I never heard of a ghost doing that!*

She traded a wide-eyed look with Camilla. Both girls ducked quickly behind the closest clump of bushes . . .

And the ghost turned around, ripping off its bonnet and tossing it on to the ground. 'I hate this,' growled a familiar male voice.

That's no ghost! Olivia realised.

It was Garrick.

She clapped her hand over her mouth to hold back a peal of laughter. The former Head Beast of Franklin Grove Middle School looked utterly miserable in his elaborate dress, with white gloves reaching up his sturdy arms and a wide hooped skirt billowing out around him.

He glared up at the sky. 'Why do *I* have to wear the dress?'

Olivia followed his gaze . . . and gulped as she spotted Josh and his cronies perched up in the trees overhead, smirking down at their friend.

'Aw, c'mon, Garrick,' Josh called back. 'You look cute!'

The rest of the greasy gang erupted into mocking laughter, and Garrick's face turned brick-red. 'I'm done,' he snarled, and stuck the parasol point-down into the ground. 'This plan is stupid!'

'Too late.' Josh's voice was suddenly harsh, his face forbidding, as he glared down at the former Beast. 'You agreed to this, just like all the rest of us. How else are we supposed to stir up some interest? This town is filling up with nosy people. All we have to do is let a few of them spot you, and they'll start talking. *Then* we can talk Gregor into coming into town to catch a glimpse of "Patience"!'

'I know,' Garrick muttered, 'but . . .'

'Don't you want to be on TV?' Josh crossed his arms. 'Don't be a baby, Garrick. All you have to do is wear a dress and run around a little, and we'll all be famous. Just think – Gregor might even let you hang out with him and his crew! Isn't that worth a little inconvenience?'

Garrick's shoulders slumped. As he mumbled his agreement, Camilla's elbow poked into Olivia's side.

'Let's get out of here,' Camilla whispered.

Olivia nodded gratefully. *Far, far away, before they notice us!*

The girls crept back through the trees as quietly as they could. When they finally stepped out on to the field, though, Camilla started to laugh uncontrollably. 'I can't believe it!' she said. 'Of all the possibilities I considered, I *never* thought those jerks could have made the whole thing up. When I think of all the time I've wasted over the last few days, researching a ghost who doesn't exist . . .!'

Olivia forced a smile. 'So you don't think there's such a thing as ghosts any more?'

Camilla threw up her hands. 'I admit it. I was completely fooled! *Eesh*, how embarrassing. I still don't know how those idiots pulled off that stunt, but now that I know it was just a prank, I can finally stop worrying about it and get back to my *real* work, just like I should have been doing all along.'

'Right,' Olivia said. 'Why don't you tell me about your new movie idea?'

But as they crossed the park and Camilla grew more and more relaxed, chattering on and on about the next movie she was planning to make, and about all the new and different camera angles that she would use for it, Olivia's smile slipped away.

The problem was, Olivia was one hundred per cent certain that the boys' prank had only started *after* the Halloween party. All it seemed like the greasy gang were doing now was exploiting what had already happened to get themselves on TV. But if she and Ivy didn't think of a solution before the famous Gregor was lured into town, Josh and Garrick's silly prank was going to turn into a mega-disaster for every vamp in Franklin Grove.

Olivia stifled a moan of frustration. *I can't believe that bunch of bozos turned out to be so smart!* If nothing else, Josh and the others knew a lot more local history than she would have expected. Even Ivy hadn't heard of the Calhoun twins' story until this week!

Maybe the adult vamps can sort it out? They must be able to stop this somehow.

'Look.' Camilla nudged her, interrupting her gloomy thoughts. 'At least we're not the only gullible ones.'

Nearby, two groups of unfamiliar adults were hurrying across the field towards the woods, their phones and tablets open to show the same map that Camilla had used to find the grounds of the Calhouns' house.

'I think it's this way!' one man called.

Another one gasped and pointed as a figure flickered between the trees. 'I saw something moving!'

Together, the two groups lunged into the woods.

Olivia sighed. 'It looks like Garrick's going running in his costume again.'

'What do you think?' Camilla said. 'Will it go viral by the end of the day? Or by the end of the hour?'

Olivia only groaned.

Chapter Seven

That night, Ivy stared at the forest of paper laid out on the kitchen table in front of her and blew air out through her lips. *This is going to take forever!* Olivia had brought everything that Camilla had collected for her investigation – print-outs of old articles, photos, obscure blog posts and Camilla's own scribbled notes and theories – all of which she had promised her friend she would throw away.

'And I *will*,' Olivia had said earlier, as she helped Ivy spread everything out on the table. 'Soon.' Then she'd rushed off to have dinner with her adoptive parents, leaving the vamps to wade through the scarily large stack of information. Even with Brendan, Sophia and Reiko all gathered at the table with her, Ivy couldn't imagine how they would ever manage to read everything.

Thank darkness there wasn't anything about the Calhouns on the World Vide Veb, at least, Ivy thought as she picked up the next piece of paper from the pile. *It's bad enough that every vampire in Franklin Grove is freaking out, without the rest of the vamp world joining in!*

She usually felt a thrill of investigative fervour when a mystery started coming together. This time, though, her shoulders felt heavier with each new piece of information she absorbed, as if the sadness of the story were physically weighing her down. With every new detail she learned, she could imagine it more clearly: the way Patience must have felt as she waited and waited – first, for her father and twin to return, and then, after she'd finally given up on that, for any news to explain what had happened to them.

If Ivy was ever worried about Olivia, all she had to do was call her twin on the phone, no matter how far apart they might be. Back in the Calhouns' time, though, there would have been no TV, no Internet – nothing to carry news swiftly across the world.

Patience must have been half-crazy with panic by the time she finally learned the truth. Ivy shuddered.

Next to Ivy, Reiko set down the printed blog entry that she'd been reading and let out a sigh. 'I know it's silly,' she said, 'but to me, the saddest part of the whole story is that obsidian bracelet that Patience is said to carry everywhere.'

'Obsidian bracelet . . .?' Ivy frowned, flicking back through the articles she'd already read. So far, she'd read more nineteenth-century history than modern ghost stories, but . . . 'I haven't seen anything about that one yet.'

'Ooh, I think I read that blog post.' Sophia

gazed broodingly at the silver bracelet on her own wrist. 'Patience planned to give the bracelet to Hope at their belated birthday tea. Apparently, whenever her ghost appears, she's always holding Hope's obsidian bracelet, as a reminder of her lost sister. Almost as if she still clings on to the idea that one day she will be able to give it to her.'

'So *that* was the birthday present that Albert mentioned this morning,' Brendan said. He frowned. 'What is obsidian, anyway?'

'Black glass from a volcano,' Sophia explained. 'It can be made into small, round beads or left in big pieces. All the people who've seen Patience say that hers is a chunky black bracelet, and –'

An unexpected voice spoke sharply behind them. 'Did you say *a chunky black bracelet*?'

Ivy swung around and saw her twin standing in the kitchen doorway. Ivy had left the front door unlocked for Olivia to let herself in after she had eaten with the Abbotts. Now she stood staring at Sophia, her blue eyes wide.

'Well . . . yes.' Sophia turned in her seat. 'Did you read the same blog post about Hope's obsidian bracelet as I did? It took me forever to track that down.'

'I haven't read any blogs about it, but . . .' Olivia swallowed visibly. 'I think I've seen the real thing.'

'What?' Frowning, Ivy hurried over to her sister. 'You look like you're about to pass out!'

'I'm fine,' said Olivia. 'My thoughts are just chasing each other, that's all.' She moved to the table, sitting down in Ivy's chair. Ivy stood behind her as she continued. 'That girl I told you about from the party – who I think might have been Patience – she was holding a bracelet just like that.'

Sophia's eyebrows rose. Olivia took a deep, shuddering breath and went on. 'Look, you guys know what happened in the park today . . .'

Ivy nodded. 'We all got your texts.'

'Good,' Olivia said. 'So we know Josh and

the other boys have really upped their game, and they're definitely exploiting any local legends they can find. But I seriously doubt that they can have uncovered that detail, considering how, even with Albert's tip, we've only just found it ourselves, buried in what Camilla had collected. Plus I don't think Garrick was wearing a bracelet in the woods today. And besides, the girl I met was definitely *not* Garrick in a dress!'

'Well . . .' Ivy tried to think clearly. 'I guess they *could* have recruited a girl to help . . .'

'No way!' Reiko said. '*Those* guys?'

'She's right,' Sophia said, her expression full of distaste. 'If you think any of those boys could talk any girl into hanging out with them . . .'

Even Ivy shuddered. 'They couldn't do it without at least taking a shower first,' she agreed.

'I can't believe a girl could ever be that gross!' said Olivia. 'But in that case . . . I really *did* talk to a ghost on Halloween.' She collapsed back into the chair, her face pale. 'What if ghosts really *are* the most rational explanation, after all?'

Sophia shook her head in wonder. 'It's really possible, isn't it? Maybe the spirit of Patience is unable to rest until she finally gives Hope her birthday gift.'

'Oh, great!' Ivy groaned. 'How is that ever going to happen?'

The table lapsed into a glum silence. Still, the idea kept turning over and over in Ivy's head. She drummed her fingers on the back of her sister's chair as she stood behind Olivia. This whole situation was totally impossible . . . but still, there was something about Sophia's idea that felt right. If nothing else, the fact that Olivia had noticed and remembered *that* detail at the party had to mean something. If Ivy could only figure out –

Ding-dong! The doorbell echoed through the house.

'Are we expecting anyone else?' Sophia asked.

'Nope.' Ivy shook her head. 'It's probably a

door-to-door salesman.' She turned to stride out of the room. 'I'll go get rid of them while you guys keep thinking.'

When she opened the front door, though, all that she could see was a massive bouquet of fat pink and white chrysanthemums right in front of her. Blinking, she took a step back, and looked at the deliveryman who stood holding the bouquet. His face was completely hidden by the mass of flowers. A big, puffy jacket protected him from the cold rain falling through the darkness outside, and she could just barely make out a baseball cap peeping over the top of the bouquet.

'Flower delivery!' the man announced in a nasal voice.

Ivy shook her head and stepped back again, starting to close the door. 'Sorry, I think you've got the wrong address. No one here ordered flowers.' *And even if they had,* she added silently, *they definitely wouldn't have ordered pink ones! Talk about bunny flowers.*

'Oh, this is definitely the right address!' The deliveryman stuck out his foot, wedging it in the doorway before she could finish closing the door. 'Perhaps if I could speak to someone else? Your sister, maybe? *Someone* must want these lovely chrysanthemums!'

Ivy gritted her teeth. 'Look –' she began.

But before she could continue, the delivery man nudged the bouquet directly into her face. '*Lovely* chrysanthemums!' he repeated loudly. 'Grown in China for over three thousand years, you know!'

Ivy recoiled, brushing the soft, smothering flowers aside. *Wait a second. How does he know I have a sister?*

'Very important in Chinese art!' he continued enthusiastically. 'And in Japan –'

'I don't –'

'– there's a whole Festival of Happiness centred around them!' He waved the bouquet triumphantly. 'Don't you want to be happy?'

That does it!

The vamps were facing exposure on national television, Ivy had spent all day imagining what it would feel like to lose her twin, and now this guy wanted her to be *happy*?

So much for being polite. Ivy's face contorted into a scowl as she aimed her most ferocious death-squint ever at the brim of the man's baseball cap. 'I won't be happy,' she snapped, 'until you take those stupid flowers away and *leave me alone!*'

The delivery man froze. Then he lowered the bouquet and peered at her, his familiar blue eyes filled with concern. The nasal twang vanished from his voice as he said, 'Hey, Ivy. Is everything OK?'

For a moment, Ivy just stared, frozen with shock. Then she burst out laughing. 'You idiot!' she said affectionately to her twin's megastar boyfriend. 'Are you *ever* going to get tired of playing dress-up?'

Jackson Caulfield laughed as he stepped inside, wrapping her in a flowery hug. 'Never,' he told her firmly. 'Now, if I can't interest you in any chrysanthemums, do you think you could take me to Olivia?'

Grinning, Ivy led him down the hallway to the kitchen. The last of her bad mood vanished as she saw her twin's face flush with excitement. 'Jackson!' Olivia jumped up and ran to fling her arms around her boyfriend. 'I can't believe you got here so quickly!'

'How could I not?' Jackson pressed his cheek against her hair and hugged her tightly, pressing the flowers into her back. 'Your invitation was just what I needed. I've been missing you too much to stay away!'

Aww. Ivy couldn't wipe away her sappy grin as she watched them. 'I didn't know you'd invited him,' she said to Olivia.

'I hadn't had a chance to tell you yet.' Still beaming, Olivia shifted to Jackson's side and took the chrysanthemums, breathing in their scent with obvious delight. 'It was my brilliant idea from this afternoon. I asked him to come, so that he can distract all our "tourists".' She glanced meaningfully at the piles of paper on the table.

'Aha!' Ivy let out a peal of laughter. 'Oh, that's perfect. Having a famous actor come to town is great misdirection!'

'Sorry?' Jackson looked at her quizzically. 'Misdirection from what, exactly? Olivia still hasn't explained. Why are all these tourists here anyway? And what exactly don't you want people to see?'

Oops. Ivy swallowed a groan as she realised just how close she'd come to making a huge mistake in her relief. Even Olivia – her own flesh and blood – hadn't been allowed to learn the secret of the vamps until she'd managed to pass some serious tests. There was no way that Jackson could be allowed to find out!

She traded a panicked look with her own boyfriend, and Brendan came to the rescue.

147

'Hey, Jackson.' He waved from the table, attracting Jackson's gaze. 'Good to see you, man.'

'You, too.' Jackson smiled and nodded to Sophia and Reiko, too, but then he turned back to Ivy. 'So . . .?'

Brendan's interruption had given Ivy just enough time to think. The truth was, Jackson spent so much time around her family, she actually forgot sometimes that he *didn't* know their real vampire identity. But this time, at least, there were very few details she had to leave out.

'It's a bunch of dumb boys from our school,' she told him. 'They're stirring up trouble and scaring people by pretending there's a ghost in town.'

'Are you serious?' Jackson let out a yelp of laughter and shook his head. 'Who actually believes in ghosts?'

Reiko coughed. Olivia winced.

Ivy said, 'Lots of people, unfortunately. And it's pulling in wannabe ghost hunters from all over the place. They're descending on the town and messing everything up. But thanks to Olivia's brilliance . . .' she grinned wickedly '. . . we have something *much* more interesting for everyone to think about now. Who wouldn't rather pay attention to a genuine Hollywood movie star?'

Jackson looked pained. 'You do know what you're asking of me, right?'

Before Ivy could answer, her twin set down her flowers and bent into a full-body stretch, as if she was getting ready for a workout.

The other vamps looked just as baffled as Ivy felt. Only Jackson looked unfazed.

'Um . . .' Ivy cleared her throat. 'Olivia? You do know, right, that it's a Saturday night? So we don't actually have to get ready for gym class right now?'

'Oh, I know,' Olivia said grimly. 'This is going to be much worse. Trust me . . .' She gave her boyfriend a knowing look. 'If our time out in public together in London was anything to go by, we'll *all* need to warm up properly if we want to outrun the paparazzi!'

All the laughter from earlier that evening felt hard to remember as Ivy tossed and turned in her coffin that night. Every time she closed her eyes, the storm outside sent a shiver down her spine. The windows rattled as if they were being shaken by ghostly hands, and the low wail of the wind sounded weirdly similar to the haunting noise that had filled Café Creative at the end of Camilla's show.

'Aargh!' Ivy pulled her black-and-red quilt over her face to muffle her own groan.

This is so embarrassing.

Scary, tough vampires were not supposed to get spooked . . . but Ivy totally was. So maybe, until they had solved their ghost problem, sleeping in a coffin might not actually be the best idea! As the windows gave another loud rattle, she swallowed down a very *un*-vamptastic squeak and jerked upright. *That's it.* Grabbing a pillow and one end of her quilt, she jumped out of the coffin and started for the door. Sleeping on the living room couch sounded like a much better option . . . as long as no one else ever found out about it!

A soft thump sounded as the end of her quilt knocked something off her casketside table. Sighing, Ivy stopped to look for whatever had fallen . . . then grimaced as she recognised the deerstalker hat she had worn on Halloween.

So much for Ivy Holmes!

There might be clues to be found all throughout Franklin Grove, but her own investigation was taking her in a direction she really didn't like.

'I *so* did not want to believe in ghosts,' Ivy muttered to the deerstalker as she placed it carefully back on the small table.

Unfortunately, they hadn't had any luck finding a girl who might have posed as Patience Calhoun on Halloween to fool Olivia, or figured out how that weird effect could have taken place at the party. But even if ghosts *were* actually real – even if Sophia was right, and they knew exactly why Patience was haunting Franklin Grove – Ivy still had no idea how to help her find peace.

Groaning, she pulled the quilt up around her shoulders and headed downstairs.

Even in the warmth of the living room, though, she couldn't fall asleep. After half an hour of trying, stretched out on the elegant black couch, she gave up and picked up the remote control from the coffee table to flick on the TV. When Lillian had first moved in, she'd insisted on getting a better cable package, with at least a hundred new channels. Now Ivy started clicking through them, grimly determined. *There has to be something here that isn't ghost-related!*

When she landed on the shopping channel, she set down the remote. 'Perfect,' she mumbled. *This will definitely put me to sleep!*

But the next moment her eyes widened and she jerked back, away from the TV.

'. . . this unusual obsidian jewellery set . . .' intoned the announcer, as the camera panned down from the matching earrings and necklace to focus on a large, heavy black bracelet.

'Aagh!' Moaning, Ivy scrambled for the remote control. The last thing she wanted was a reminder of the ghostly mystery!

She let out a breath of relief as she clicked on to the next station, where the local news anchors were droning through a weather report. A repeat of tonight's news show. *This has to be better.*

And it was . . . until one of the anchors grinned and said, 'So, Jenny, I hear little Franklin Grove is getting an unusual visitor?'

'That's right, Bob. The famous Gregor Gleka, aka "the Ghost Grabber", is apparently determined to investigate the strange goings-on that have been reported in the small town ever since Halloween.'

The other news anchor smirked and waggled her fingers. 'Sounds spooky to me! What do you think, Bob? Could there really be ghosts in Franklin Grove?'

'I don't want to hear it!' Ivy wailed. She turned the TV off with a *click* and slammed the remote back down on the coffee table.

Then she drew up her knees and tucked herself into a ball at one end of the couch, pulling the warm quilt up around her. Burying her head against her knees, she let out a low groan of frustration in the quiet darkness.

'Ivy?' Her dad's voice spoke just behind her.

Gasping, Ivy jumped up, letting the quilt fall to the floor.

Charles stood in the doorway, wearing elegant black silk pyjamas and a crimson dressing gown and rubbing his eyes with the back of one hand. His hair stood up in every direction.

'Wow, Dad.' Her shoulders relaxing, Ivy nearly

smiled. 'That's some epic coffin head you've got!'

'Very funny.' Charles dropped his hand and narrowed his eyes. 'But I want to know about you. What's brought you down here at this time of night?'

'Oh . . .' Ivy wrapped her arms around her chest, looking away from her father's searching expression. 'I'm fine. You should go back to bed. Don't worry. Everything's OK.'

Shaking his head, Charles walked into the room. 'I can tell that it's not.' His face grave, he sat down on the couch and patted the seat for Ivy to sit down beside him. 'Have you been worrying about our ghost issue? I'm sorry. I know you've seen how concerned I am . . . but just because I take these problems seriously doesn't mean I expect you to solve them for me! Believe it or not, you know, you really are only fourteen years old. No one expects you to take charge of protecting our community.'

Sighing, Ivy leaned her head against his

shoulder. 'I'd love to be able to give up and stop worrying,' she admitted. 'But now that I'm so far into the investigation . . . I just can't.' She turned her head to peer up at him. 'Do you understand? I can't bear to stop now, before I've figured it all out. That's just not the way I'm made.'

'I understand.' Smiling ruefully, Charles dropped a kiss on her forehead. 'And do you know what? I'll tell you a secret: that unwillingness of yours to palm off responsibility is actually one of the qualities that makes me most proud to be your father. But . . .' He gave her a stern look as he stood up. 'That doesn't mean you should stop looking after yourself, too. Understood? I want you to get *some* sleep tonight!'

'Understood,' Ivy said. 'Goodnight, Dad.'

She was smiling as he left the room . . . but the smile was wiped off her face only a moment later when the windows gave a sudden, massive rattle.

'*Ahhhhhhhhhhh . . .*'

It was that wailing wind again! It made every

inch of her spine prickle. Driven by instinct, Ivy ran in a blur of vampiric speed to the window. She pushed open the curtains . . . and a chill ran through her as she glimpsed a girl in a long, Victorian-style dress walking slowly down the street. But this dress wasn't red – it was a pale blue. Ivy couldn't tell from this angle whether the girl was carrying any obsidian jewellery in her hands, but as she watched, the wide skirts of the girl's dress seemed to shine and shimmer in the faint light of the street lamps.

Ivy clenched the windowsill in both hands, forcing herself to take deep breaths. *It could just be a coincidence . . . or Garrick in a different dress . . . or . . . or . . .*

But even as she scrambled to find any believable explanation, she noticed something spookier yet.

As the strange girl disappeared into the shadows of Undertaker Hill, the air outside fell completely silent.

The wailing wind was gone.

Chapter Eight

Olivia took a deep breath as she stepped into the front hallway of her house the next morning. She was wearing her most comfortable shoes and a pair of grey yoga pants under a long pink sweater. She'd tucked her cell phone and wallet into a small, blue cross-body bag that couldn't possibly fall off, no matter how fast she moved. She'd even pinned her long hair up into a messy topknot to protect it from being yanked.

'Are you ready?' Jackson was waiting by the front door, looking impossibly gorgeous in a deep blue sweater and fitted jeans.

'Almost.' Testing the cross-body bag, Olivia did

a quick lunge . . . then nodded firmly. 'There!' She started for the door. 'I'm as warmed up as I'll ever be. When we have to run, I won't let you down.'

'Believe me, I was never worried about that.' Smiling, Jackson reached out to take her hand. 'You didn't let me down in London, did you, when we had to run from the hordes there?'

'Yes, well, that was sheer panic taking over,' Olivia admitted. 'Back then, I didn't really understand what we were in for!'

Squeezing his hand, she took a deep breath and opened the door.

Then she blinked. *Wait a second. Where are the crowds?*

Admittedly, it was still early on a Sunday morning, and Olivia's street was usually sleepy even at peak times. But surely the news of Jackson's arrival must have spread around Franklin Grove by now! There should have been crowds of teenagers bursting from their homes, screaming their heads off. Olivia had even updated her Twitter feed that morning with news of her "surprise visitor", to make sure all Jackson's fans could easily guess where he was.

Jackson just shrugged. 'Maybe we need to go somewhere a bit more public.'

'Let's hit the Food Mart,' Olivia decided. 'We'll definitely be noticed there!'

And they needed to be noticed right away . . . because just five minutes before they'd left the house, Olivia had gotten a frantic text message from Ivy. Gregor Gleka was making his way to Franklin Grove *right now*. There wasn't a moment to lose!

Pinning a bright smile to her face, Olivia walked with Jackson down the main street of Franklin Grove and into the Food Mart, or rather – as it would definitely become as soon as Jackson's fans spotted them – the Scream Zone. *Ivy's really going to owe me for this!* she thought. The aisles in the Food

Mart were narrow enough that if a swarm of Jackson's fans descended on them, they might well get trampled!

Holding hands, Olivia and Jackson strolled down the aisles, doing one full lap of the grocery store . . . and then another.

Olivia stared at the oblivious shoppers all around them. Then she pulled out her phone, scrolling through her Twitter feed. 'Doesn't *anyone* have a smartphone?' she demanded. 'I can't believe we're out in public, and not a single person has tweeted about it. This place should be a zoo by now! Where are all the screaming girls?'

Jackson looked sheepish. 'I have to admit, I don't really miss them,' he said. He gave Olivia a mischievous grin. 'Hey, maybe my star is finally falling. That might not bode well for *Eternal Sunset*, but it would make it a lot easier for us to go out on a date!'

'Your star is definitely not falling,' Olivia said

firmly. 'How many magazine covers have you been on in the last two months?'

'Well . . .' He shrugged, looking embarrassed. 'Maybe a couple.'

'More like four or five.' Olivia rolled her eyes. 'Maybe it's just because you spent a good amount of time here last year, going to school like a regular kid. That could explain why people in Franklin Grove don't freak out any more.'

The middle-aged cashier at the check-out line nodded calmly to Jackson as they passed her for a second time. 'Looking forward to the new movie, young man!'

'Thank you, ma'am.' He gave her a sweet smile. 'I hope you enjoy it!'

Olivia sighed as they started their third lap of the store. 'At least *someone* cares you're here.'

'Sorry,' Jackson said. 'I know it's not what you were hoping for . . . but it is actually nice to feel normal for once.'

'I bet.' Olivia touched his arm sympathetically with her free hand. 'But it's not going to help us outwit that Ghost Grabber man, is it?'

Before Jackson could answer, a sudden murmur of excitement rippled across the Food Mart. As Olivia watched, shoppers from all across the store started racing towards the front door.

'Uh-oh.' Olivia hurried after them, pulling Jackson with her.

Shoppers lined the glass windows at the front of the store, chattering excitedly and snapping pictures with their phones. Olivia wriggled her way to the front of the crowd just as a crimson hearse rolled past the store at a funereally slow pace. Plastered on the side of the hearse, painted three times larger than life, was . . .

'Looks like the Grabber's here,' Jackson murmured into her ear.

Olivia winced as she watched the picture of Gregor Gleka's face – his eyes wide in mock

163

horror – roll past on the side of the hearse. There was no way that anybody in Franklin Grove was going to miss the Ghost Grabber's arrival.

Jackson nudged her as more camera flashes exploded around them. 'It sure looks like people are excited about *this*!' He let out a low whistle. 'I don't know how good he is with ghosts, but this old guy is definitely "grabbing" my *thunder*.'

Olivia wanted to laugh along with him, but she couldn't. 'This is a disaster! He's going all out. That means he really is going to devote a whole episode of his show to Franklin Grove. Everyone will know about it! People are going to be *interested*, and then they'll start asking *questions*, and . . .' She cut herself off with a gasp as she suddenly realised what she'd been saying.

Jackson was frowning at her, his gaze intent. 'Who cares if people ask questions?' he asked. 'Seriously, what are you so worried about?'

'Um . . .' Olivia's head went blank as she stared back at him. 'Uh . . .'

'It's not like there's anything you're trying to hide,' Jackson said slowly, '. . . is there?'

Uh-oh. With a gulp, Olivia forced herself to think fast. 'Of course not!' she said. Her words rattled out too quickly, and she could hear her voice turning high-pitched and squeaky, but she forced herself onwards anyway. 'I just hate the idea of ghosts, you know? And this is such a small town. If a whole TV crew shows up, it'll be a nightmare zone for days. People won't stop griping about it for months!' She forced a tinkling laugh that sounded super-fake even to her own ears. 'I mean, who wants that hassle, right?'

She could hear her own heartbeat thumping in her ears as she stared at Jackson, waiting for his response.

He just peered at her. 'It didn't bother you when *The Groves* was being filmed here.'

'I know!' Olivia replied. Excuses chased explanations in her brain. 'But that was . . . different.'

'How so?' Jackson's eyes narrowed.

He's totally suspecting something now, Olivia thought, wishing there was a button she could push that would divert the rushing blood away from her face.

'Well,' she said at last. '*You* were working on *The Groves*. If you were co-hosting the Ghost Grabber's show, then I might be more excited!'

Jackson stared at her a moment longer. Then he smiled. 'O . . . K,' he said.

But she could sense his thoughtful frown even as she turned away.

🦇　　🦇　　🦇

Anyone would think this was a military operation, Ivy thought, as she stood opposite the Meat and Greet, scowling at the chaos in front of her. A whole battalion of TV production trucks were lined up in front of the diner, surrounded by a swarm of busy-looking people yelling into handsets and cell phones.

'Apparently, this is just the pre-production phase,' Sophia said, reading the stream of updates on her slim black phone, 'Gleka's commandeering the whole diner for his show. It's going to be the site of an impromptu "Ghost Chat"' – she made finger-quotes as she read the words out loud – 'in which he plans to "make contact" with the "Ghost of the Grove".'

'Seriously?' Brendan snorted with laughter. 'I've never seen a place less likely to attract a ghost! Come on, it's full of bright lights, people, chatter . . . unless our Victorian ghost turns out to like cheeseburgers and fries, I'm pretty sure Gleka'll be out of luck!'

'Right . . .' Ivy's attempt at a laugh almost choked her.

So far she hadn't told anyone about the girl she'd seen outside her window last night. She wasn't used to being creeped out by anything, but she couldn't make herself talk about it calmly yet, either. And no matter how hard she wanted to think it had just been Garrick in a dress, she couldn't convince herself.

'The problem is,' she said, 'what if he really does uncover something? If *that* happens –'

Reiko pinched her arm hard, cutting her off.

'Shut it down!' Sophia hissed at the same moment. She nodded her head meaningfully at the couple walking down the street towards them.

Oops. Ivy nodded in agreement as she recognised Jackson walking hand-in-hand with Olivia. 'Right,' she whispered. 'From now on, everyone talk in code.'

The whole group fell into awkward silence as Olivia and Jackson joined them.

'Hey,' Jackson said. 'You guys all look like you just got bad news. Seriously. Did this guy Gleka kick someone's dog or something?'

'Um . . .' Ivy slid a nervous glance at Brendan, who gave a tight smile and a shrug in return. 'We'd just like to get into the Meat and Greet early, to guarantee that we get a good seat in the audience,' she said. 'Just to make sure nothing too, uh, *annoying* happens.'

'Like . . .?' Jackson prompted. His million-dollar smile slipped into a serious discount zone when the vampires stayed silent. 'OK, I don't remember the Grovers being *quite* this secretive back when I was one of you guys. Is something up that you don't want to tell me? You can trust me, of all people, not to go blabbing to the newspapers.'

'Oh, we know,' Ivy said. 'It's just . . .' She trailed off, searching for an excuse.

'Plus,' Jackson added, 'aren't I supposed to be running interference on the crowds? So I *should* know what's going on, right?'

Ivy traded a desperate glance with Olivia, who looked pained.

169

Jackson's smile lost a few more dollars as he waited. Finally, he sighed and shrugged. 'Fine. If it's important to you guys, I'll do what I can to help. I won't even ask any more questions. Once this is all over, though, I'm serious – I'd really like to know what I'm helping you *with*. Got it?'

'Got it,' Ivy agreed with a smile of pure relief.

Some day soon, she knew she'd start to panic about how to come up with a story that Jackson might actually buy as an explanation . . . but right now, she was just glad not to have to deal with that problem on top of all the rest.

First things first!

'OK then. Let's see what we can do.' Reaching into his pocket, Jackson pulled out a pair of Hollywood-worthy sunglasses. He slipped them on and his whole posture shifted, turning aloof and untouchable. 'Follow my lead,' he muttered out of the side of the mouth. Then he started across the street, heading for the throng of busy-looking TV crew members in front of the line of trucks.

'Dude!' He slapped the closest man on the back, startling him into lowering his cell phone. 'Jackson Caulfield,' he drawled, and gave a smirk. 'You might have heard of me?'

'Uh . . . wow . . . Wow! *Jackson*!' The man shut down his phone, as other crew members flocked towards them, drawn by Jackson's familiar face. 'What are you doing here, man? Shouldn't you be partying in LA right now?'

'Nah. LA's so *tired* this time of year,' Jackson said, in a weary tone of voice Ivy had never heard from him before. 'I mean, the whole place is so totally last season, isn't it? No, I like gathering up my buddies' – he nodded to Ivy and the others – 'and spending *my* free time somewhere new. Unspoiled. Looks like your boss feels the same!' He pointed at the diner. 'Word on the street is, you guys are shooting in there today. I'm a huge fan of the Ghost Grabber, man. Any chance I could watch the master at work?'

'Well . . .' The man in front of him traded a wary look with the other crew members around him. 'I'm not sure. I mean . . .'

The woman behind him pushed forwards, holding a clipboard tightly against her chest as if to keep its contents secret. 'You aren't thinking of, like, *playing* Gregor in some TV movie or something about his life, are you?'

Is she serious? Ivy had to turn her head to hide her laughter. *Like Jackson Caulfield is going to do a TV movie any time soon . . .much less about Gregor Gleka!*

Jackson only smiled enigmatically, his blue eyes hidden behind his sunglasses. 'Obviously, I can't talk about any projects I might or might not have in the pipeline. My agent would have a fit if I shared any secrets. But . . .' He gestured towards Olivia and the others. 'Y'know, my entourage and I . . .'

Did he just call us his entourage? Ivy narrowed her eyes at her sister's boyfriend. *Oh, he is enjoying this way too much!*

'. . . would see it as a personal favour,' Jackson continued smoothly, 'if we could be on-set for Gregor's special. To, like, soak up the vibe.'

'Oh, wow,' the man breathed. 'Seriously?'

'Got it,' said the woman briskly. 'No promises, but we'll see what we can do.' Spinning on one heel, she pulled out her walkie-talkie and started barking orders into it. 'We need a special favour here . . .'

Up and down the line of trucks, whispers and excited chatter broke out as the news spread.

'Jackson Caulfield!' Ivy heard someone gasp.

Gotcha. Ivy wanted to crow with triumph, but settled for a satisfied smirk.

Stepping away from the trucks, Jackson grinned at the group of vamps and Olivia. 'I'll be happy to accept my fee in video games, gratitude, smoothies and worship, thank you.'

'Yeah, right. I'm warning you, Caulfield . . .' Ivy gave him a mock-death-squint. 'You get away with calling me part of your "entourage" *once*. But not twice!'

Laughing, Jackson gave her a sharp salute. 'Got it, General Vega!'

As the female crew member hurried towards them, a broad smile on her face, Ivy's shoulders relaxed. *This is really going to happen.*

Thank darkness that Olivia had such an unquestioningly loyal boyfriend! But all the same . . .

She slid him a sidelong glance as they walked into the crowded diner.

How long are we going to be able to keep our secret from Jackson, now that he's finally asking questions?

🦇   🦇   🦇

Ten minutes later, though, Ivy had bigger worries on her mind. 'Ugh!' She nudged Olivia as they stood in a group by the counter, watching the preparations for the shoot. 'Seriously, how do you not go batty sitting through this kind of thing

every day when you're working?' she whispered.
'I've only been on the set of *The Ghost Grabber
Special* for, like, four minutes, and I'm ready to die
of boredom!'

Olivia sniffed. 'At least on my sets,' she
whispered back, 'I know I'm making something
good! Plus, the people are a whole lot nicer. Just
look at him!' Surreptitiously, she pointed at Gregor
Gleka himself, who was in the middle of shouting
at a cowering assistant.

'You're supposed to take out all the *purple* Skittles
before you hand me the bag!' Gleka bellowed. 'Not
the green ones! I love the green Skittles!'

'Whoa.' Ivy raised her eyebrows. 'Talk about
someone who's scarier than real ghosts!'

Olivia snickered and turned to whisper
something in Jackson's ear.

Ivy looked around the diner, shaking her head
in disbelief. It looked so different, she could barely
even recognise it. All the usual tables had been

cleared out, leaving only a wide, heavy-looking circular one, brought in by Gleka's crew and placed in the centre of the room. As she watched, two assistants wrestled with a heavy, blood-red tablecloth. Around the room, other crew members were busy setting up lights and debating loudly about what might be the "eeriest angles".

Ivy rolled her eyes.

As Jackson was lured away to sign autographs for various crew members' children, Reiko turned to Ivy. Today, her hair was a deep crimson that perfectly matched the rest of the set, but her expression was blatantly sceptical. 'Not to raise the obvious question,' she muttered, 'but do we even have a plan?'

Ivy winced. 'Not really. I was sort of hoping that something would come to me once I was in here.'

'Hmm.' Sophia huddled in to share the whispered consultation. 'Are you thinking sabotage?'

'I was considering finding the fuse box and causing a power shortage,' Ivy admitted, 'but the problem is, that would ruin any food in the diner's freezers. I don't want to shut down one of my favourite places!'

'Definitely not,' Brendan agreed. 'I don't want to live in a world without the Meat and Greet!' He frowned as he looked over Ivy's head at Gregor Gleka. 'What if we just take advantage of being on-screen as an audience? When no ghosts show up, we could point and laugh – make it really clear that Gregor's crazy. He'd be way too embarrassed to use that footage for his special!'

'I'm not sure that would be enough.' Ivy sighed. 'I just wish we could offer him an obvious *explanation* for why a ghost in an old-timey dress has been wandering around everywhere. If we could only . . . oh. *Oh*!'

Before she could think twice, Ivy grabbed Olivia, pulling her sister into their group huddle. 'I think I've finally got a plan!' she hissed. 'It's totally insane, and if it doesn't work this could turn into the most embarrassing day of our entire lives – but honestly, I think that it's our only shot!'

Olivia didn't miss a beat. 'OK . . . I'm listening.'

Ivy looked to Sophia, pointing to the stylish white leather handbag over her shoulder. 'You don't happen to have any pale foundation in there, do you?'

🦇   🦇   🦇

Twenty minutes later, Ivy watched from the sidelines as filming began on *Gregor's Ghost Chat*. Black drapes had been placed over all the windows to make it look as if Gregor were working at night as he sat at the heavy, round table in the centre of the room, surrounded by locals Ivy vaguely recognised from the streets of Franklin Grove.

All the audience members' faces were shadowed, though, as a spotlight shone straight on Gregor. The "Ghost Grabber" leaned towards the camera, his eyes haunted and his fake-Eastern-European accent clinging thickly to his words.

'I, Gregor Gleka, have been summoned to this place by the terror of ordinary people forced to confront the reality of the dark . . . People who can no longer deny the possibility of spectral phenomena in their own small-town lives, after the unsettling paranormal incidents that they have witnessed. These brave townsfolk sitting around me now have seen the ghostly girl who brought me here. She has haunted this town for years, but her recent appearance this past Halloween has *really* put the town on edge . . .'

Lights panned over the excited-looking locals at his table, and Ivy stifled a snort. *Yeah, right.* She hadn't seen a single one of those guys at Camilla's party. *In other words, they're liars who just want to get on TV!*

Or at least . . . She swallowed hard. She *hoped* they were liars. If there'd been another ghostly incident on Halloween that she didn't know about, the vamps might be in real trouble!

'Clearly,' Gregor intoned, 'this ghost must have desperately important unfinished business, to keep her here.'

Well, there's a revelation. Ivy rolled her eyes. *All* ghosts had unfinished business! Otherwise, what was the point of being a ghost? She'd bet anything that Gregor didn't even know about the obsidian bracelet that Patience still carried around for Hope. He was such a faker, he probably had no idea what it would really feel like to lose a twin, or . . .

Wait a minute! Ivy sucked in a breath. Suddenly, it was all so clear. She knew *exactly* what needed to be done to help Patience!

But not yet. She forced herself to contain her excitement. *First, we have to debunk this whole story, and turn all the suspicious eyes* away *from Franklin Grove.*

'My friends . . .' Gregor nodded solemnly to the locals around him. 'Please place your palms flat on the table, while I see if I can communicate with the spirits.' As the others pressed their hands against the table, he closed his eyes and tipped his face back – to help the camera catch every angle, Ivy was certain.

'Spirits!' Gleka's voice boomed out. 'I beseech you! Show pity on this frightened town. Commune with me now, and let me ease your pain. Spirits! Do you hear me? Spirits –'

But before he could ask another question, an eerie knocking echoed through the room.

Gregor's eyes flew open. The locals around him rustled with sudden panic.

Go, Olivia! Ivy let out a silent cheer. Her twin was doing exactly what they'd planned, even sooner than she'd expected. *Time for the sabotage to begin!*

But then a voice spoke, powerful but muffled as if it were coming through a wall, or from a different dimension – and *much, much too deep* to belong to Ivy's sister.

'We are here, Gregor Gleka!' the deep male

voice intoned. 'But why have you disturbed our immortal slumber?'

Oh my darkness! Ivy exchanged panicked looks with her friends.

If that wasn't Olivia . . . *who was it?*

Chapter Nine

The guests around Gregor's table broke out in a sudden babble of panic, their chairs scraping back as they started up as if to run.

'My friends!' Gregor held out one hand to stop them. By the glare of the bright stage spotlight, Ivy could see sudden beads of perspiration on his forehead, but his voice was commanding. 'You don't need to flee. Ghosts cannot harm the living. They are only a presence –'

The deep, ominous voice cut him off before he could finish. 'Oh, we have *presents* for you, Gregor Gleka . . .'

Wait a minute. Ivy's eyebrows lowered into a

frown. *Is that the sound of snickering in the distance?*

Thinking past her first panic, she closed her eyes and focused all of her hyper-alert vampire senses on the space around her. A moment later, her nose twitched.

I know that stink!

She narrowed her eyes at the kitchen door. The smell was definitely coming from behind there.

That's no ghost. It's Josh and his greasy gang!

'I – I would be happy to accept any gifts that you have to offer, spirits!' Gregor said. His voice was trembling now, his cheeks flushing with what looked like a mixture of excitement and fear.

I bet he thinks this is the first time he's really spoken to a ghost! Ivy shook her head despairingly. *If only he knew . . .*

That's it. Thinking fast, she grabbed Sophia's arm. Now that she knew that Josh and his gang were involved, her plan needed updating. 'Head for the kitchen door,' she whispered, 'and wait for my nod.'

'Got it.' Sophia started sidling along the edges of the room. Before anyone could notice her, Ivy ran forwards – straight for the round table where filming was taking place.

'Gregor!' she yelled. Cameras swung around to face her, and she tried her hardest to channel any acting power she might have learned from her sister. *Look like a damsel in distress*, she ordered herself, *not a tough girl!* Blinking hard, as if she were trying not to cry, she forced her voice to wobble. 'I can't take this any more! It's all too much!'

'Now, young lady . . .' Gregor began.

Ivy stomped one booted foot and brushed a hand over her eyes as she pretended to wipe away tears. 'You don't understand how *frightening* it is to live like this!' she wailed. 'Can't you do something? Like, maybe, drive it out of town?' She sniffed loudly. She regretted it, though, when she caught a whiff of Josh and his cronies. *They're still lurking . . .*

185

She shook her head, trying to stay focused on her performance. 'Everyone here is so scared, whether they want to admit it or not! Won't you save us? Please?'

'I – well, I suppose I could. Yes, why not?' Obviously, the desire for fame and glory had overcome Gregor's momentary fear. Eyes wild, he pointed at one of his assistants. 'Get me my notebooks,' he hissed. 'Now! And as for you . . .' He gave the camera crew a venomous look. 'I'm warning you, your batteries had *better* be fully charged this time. If anything goes wrong and it's your fault, you'll be out on the street before you can say the word "ghost"!'

His upper lip lifted in a snarl. 'I'm telling you, this is my big chance. If we get all the right angles on this, we might actually graduate to *real* TV. I am *not* staying on Channel 237 forever . . . The only question is whether or not I let you any of you guys come with me!'

'Yes, Gregor,' the crew all chorused glumly.

Ivy forced herself not to roll her eyes in disgust. *Think damsel. Think damsel . . .* she reminded herself.

'Now, then!' As the locals settled back into place around the table, Gregor's assistant hurried back to him. Gregor snatched the notebooks from her and shuffled through them. 'I have the perfect incantation – and as for you, young lady . . .' He gave Ivy a sickly-sweet, condescending smile. 'Yes, yes, you'll be the perfect one to help me on-camera. A frightened young girl, who I save by driving away the spirits . . . oh, the audience will love that. *Very* good for ratings!'

As the other locals frowned and rustled, Gregor beckoned Ivy to his side and handed her the notebook. 'Hold this open for me while I read the incantation, and I promise you' – he swept a triumphant look around the room – 'this time, the ghosts really will appear before our very eyes!'

'Yes, Gregor,' Ivy murmured obediently. She

pinned her lips firmly closed to keep herself from grinning.

Oh, they'll appear, all right.

As Ivy held out the notebook, Gregor began to recite a chant in a language that Ivy was horrified to recognise as Romanian, the language of Transylvania. The words rolled out impressively in Gregor's deep voice, but she had to stop herself from laughing as she realised that they made absolutely no sense when they were spoken together. Ivy was pretty sure she heard, 'Spirits swimming with tomatoes and telephones.'

I don't think that's what he meant to say!

Gregor's voice grew louder and louder with every meaningless phrase, while his accent grew thicker and his gestures more wild. Ivy let his words flow over her as she peered with her powerful vamp vision into the darkness outside the spotlight. There, in the shadows, past the rest of the crew, was . . .

Yes! Sophia stood just beside the kitchen door, her eyes on Ivy, waiting for her cue.

'. . . Spirits!' Gregor finished, switching to English in a bellow that ruffled Ivy's hair. *'Reveal yourselves!'*

'Look!' Ivy yelled, flinging out her arm to point straight at the kitchen door.

The cameras swung around to follow her pointing finger . . .

. . . just as Sophia yanked open the door, and Josh and the rest of the greasy gang fell through it.

'Woooooooh! Woooooooh!' Hooting like ghosts and laughing like maniacs, the boys didn't even seem to care that they'd been caught.

Today, none of them wore a Victorian dress. Instead, they were all covered in basic white bedsheets . . . and from the way Garrick and the others crashed into each other as they stumbled about, they seemed to have forgotten to cut themselves any eyeholes.

'*Woooooh!*'

'*Woooooooh!*'

'Oh, man, your *faces*!' cried Josh, the only one who had remembered his eyeholes. 'You all look like total idiots!'

Garrick pushed off his bedsheet to grin straight at Gregor, whose face was puce with outrage. 'Are we gonna be on TV?'

'*This . . . is . . . unbelievable*!' Gregor roared. 'You – you – you *little* . . .' His Eastern European accent vanished in an instant, his voice turning New York-nasal. 'Do you have any idea just what you've done? This is serious work! It's –'

'*Wooooooooooooohhhh*!' the boys chorused together, speaking over him. '*Watch us flyyyyyyy*!'

As the whole Meat and Greet filled with laughter, the boys leaped forwards and started racing around the room, flapping their white bedsheets.

Roaring with fury, Gregor chased after them.

Shaking her head, Ivy slipped back to the

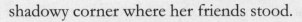

shadowy corner where her friends stood.

'I have to admit . . .' Jackson let out a relieved chuckle. 'I was actually worried there for a second that a real ghost might be putting in an appearance. Stupid, huh?'

'Mmm,' Ivy replied noncommittally, trying not to look suspicious.

More and more people joined Gregor in chasing the "ghosts" around the room, but the camera crew he'd insulted earlier just kept on filming, grinning as they turned their cameras to catch every one of their boss's near-misses. Reiko bounced up and down as she watched, cheering on different crew members as they came close to finally catching the ghosts . . . then cheering for the ghosts, too, when they escaped yet again.

Even Jackson grinned and called out encouragement.

Unlike the others, though, Ivy couldn't quite relax and enjoy the chaos yet . . . because she was pretty sure that someone else should be putting in an appearance right about now.

It's time. Walking towards the back entrance of the Meat and Greet, Olivia took a deep breath . . . or at least, as deep a breath as she could manage in the tight corset she was currently wearing. *I hope Ivy's plan is not actually as crazy as it sounded at first!*

She'd had to run all the way to the Franklin Grove Museum to borrow a red Victorian dress, but at least this time she'd been smart enough to wear trainers . . . and Albert had been more than happy to loan the historic dress when he'd heard the reason she needed it. Now that she was perfectly dressed for her part, she arranged her long hair down over her face, which she had slathered with Sophia's pale foundation. Still, she'd never felt quite so self-conscious about any part she'd ever played.

Talk about immersing yourself in a role!

This might well turn out to be the most excruciatingly embarrassing scene of her life . . . but when the vampire community really needed her, she couldn't possibly say no. *I have to protect my family, no matter what it takes.*

Head lowered to keep her face hidden under her hair, she started for the back door of the diner . . . then stopped.

Why was it standing open already?

She hurried through the doorway, her wide, floor-length skirts rustling around her. When she walked through the empty kitchen, she found that door open, too . . . and total chaos in the shadowed front room of the diner.

Olivia stared in shock as Gregor and almost all of the other crewmembers chased after five boy-shaped white "ghosts" in bedsheets. Laughter and shouting echoed around the big room. Reiko was pumping her fist in the air, Jackson was clapping . . . Only Ivy had her eyes on the kitchen doorway, and she gave Olivia a wink as she opened her mouth and raised one finger to point.

'Look!' Ivy screamed, so loudly that everyone turned.

That's my cue.

Assuming a wistful, distant look, Olivia drifted slowly through the doorway into the room.

'Ahhhh!' White bedsheets went flying as the boys threw them off.

Olivia wasn't even the slightest bit surprised to recognise Josh and his greasy gang underneath. But when they caught sight of her, their faces went sickly green.

'It's a *real* ghost!' Garrick shrieked. 'Get out of here!'

Josh lunged for the door. 'I'm getting out first – I'm your leader!'

As all five boys scrambled for the front door, Olivia kept her expression as distant and unaffected as if she hadn't heard a word they'd said. Slo-o-owly, she drifted towards Gregor, who stood frozen, staring at her as if transfixed.

Then he suddenly jumped into action. 'You!' He jabbed his fingers at the camera crew, his Eastern European accent even thicker than Olivia had heard it before. 'You had better still be rolling!' he bellowed. 'We can edit out the last few minutes. Just don't lose any of this good stuff!'

Turning back to Olivia, he smoothed down his hair and took a deep breath. 'I . . . that is . . .' He squared his shoulders. 'Spirit, I greet you,' he said to her as she drifted almost close enough to touch. Then he tilted his chin, taking the perfect angle for the camera, as he spoke towards the closest cameraman. 'I can hardly believe it. For the first time in my life, I am standing next to an actual spirit, and the feeling is almost indescribable. The –'

'Sorry, what?' Olivia giggled and hurried forwards to touch his arm, making him jump. 'Wait, no! Did you really think I was an actual ghost?'

Gregor stared at her, his jaw working up and down but no sound coming out.

Olivia threw her hair back to reveal her face and did her best ditz impression. 'I'm so *happy*!' She beamed at him. 'What a compliment! See, I'm an actress' – she fluttered her eyelashes – 'and I'm preparing for a really big role in a film called *Eternal Sunset*. Have you heard of it?'

Out of the corner of her eye, she glimpsed Jackson clapping one hand to his mouth before he turned away, his shoulders shaking with barely-restrained laughter.

Gregor swallowed visibly. 'Well – yes, but –'

'Oh, *yay*!' Olivia bounced on her toes and clapped her hands together in fake-delight. 'That is just so totally awesome! And see, the last time we were filming, my director told me something about . . . oh, I think he called it *method acting*?' She tilted her head, trying to look confused. 'Have you heard of that one, too?'

Gregor's shoulders slumped in obvious despair. 'Yes,' he groaned. 'I've heard of it.'

'Oh, you *are* smart,' Olivia said approvingly. 'So you'll understand this perfectly! Because that whole "method acting" idea got me thinking about how walking around in my costume here in my hometown would be such a great way to, like, *possess* my character. But I didn't think for one minute that I would ever scare anybody . . . This is all a big misunderstanding!' She clicked her tongue sympathetically, giving his arm another pat. 'I am just so sorry if I frightened you, Gregor. This is *sooooooo* embarrassing. I really couldn't be sorrier!'

'Oh, no?' Gregor demanded. He stared at her, eyes wide, trembling with visible outrage. 'Well, *I* am! I am sorrier than anyone can possibly imagine that I was ever fooled into visiting this town in the first place. I am never coming back here again!'

With a roar, he threw his mic to the floor. Then he collapsed beside it, burying his head in his hands, as the grinning camera crew moved closer to circle him, filming every angle of his despair.

'I can't believe it,' Gregor groaned, his voice almost unrecognisable. 'My big break – ruined! I'm never getting off Channel 237. I'm surrounded by idiots and frauds. Surrounded!'

The closest cameraman rolled his eyes, but Olivia cringed. She couldn't help feeling a little guilty . . . until suddenly, she realised something.

Wait a second. Her eyes narrowed. *He's talking in a New York accent, not an Eastern European one! Talk about a serious fraud!*

Chapter Ten

But although Gregor had been driven away, Olivia wasn't finished with ghosts yet. That night, she shivered and wrapped her arms around herself as she walked with Ivy through the moonlit skate park, towards the picnic tables and the shadows of the forest beyond. Thank goodness she had changed out of the fusty Victorian dress hours ago, back into her comfortable yoga pants and cosy sweater. But even the warm wool coat that she'd added on top didn't stop the chill that ran through her now.

'I'm not saying this is a *bad* idea,' she muttered, 'but so far, it's not my favourite of your schemes, Ivy

Vega. Are you finally ready to explain why it was so important for me to meet you in the park *at night*?'

The text that Ivy had sent her half an hour ago had been an SOS, so Olivia hadn't even bothered to argue. She just grabbed her coat and ran. But from the moment she'd met Ivy at the gates and stepped into the darkened park, leaving all the street lamps behind, her personal creep-factor had zoomed way out of control.

'We need to do this at night so that we can be alone,' Ivy told her. 'I finally figured it all out today . . . and believe it or not, it was that idiot Gregor Gleka who made me see it!' Ivy squared her shoulders. 'Do you remember that theory of Sophia's, about the final birthday tea party that the Calhoun twins were never able to celebrate?'

Olivia frowned. 'The one they were supposed to share after Hope got home from England?'

'That's right.' Ivy took long strides that swept the billowing tails of her calf-length coat out around her as they neared the picnic tables and the rustling trees just beyond. 'And remember that obsidian bracelet that Patience was holding when you saw her? The bracelet she'd been planning to give Hope at their birthday party?'

Olivia shivered. 'How could I not remember my one and only encounter with a real ghost? I couldn't forget that bracelet if I tried.'

Ivy nodded, her long hair swishing around her face in the darkness. 'What if Patience can't, either? What if Sophia was right, and giving that final gift is so important to her that she hasn't been able to rest until Hope finally gets it?'

Olivia nibbled on her lower lip, thinking it through. 'It makes sense,' she admitted at last, 'at least as much sense as any ghost story can . . . But it's just like you said to Sophia last night: what good does it do for us to know that? Hope's never going to get that gift, is she? And there's nothing we can do about it.'

'Well, that's what I used to think, too.' Ivy sighed. 'But then I saw Hope outside my house last night.'

'You did?' Olivia frowned. 'Why didn't you tell me she was in Franklin Grove too?'

Ivy shrugged, looking sheepish. 'I was too creeped out. But then I realised . . . you and I are the only two people who've actually seen the ghosts this time around. It can't be a coincidence that we were the ones they came to. Maybe Patience appearing to you is what made it possible for Hope to appear to me?'

'You mean . . .' Olivia's eyes widened. 'Because we're twins, too?'

'That's right. We're the only ones who really know what that bond feels like. And that's why we're the only ones who can do this.' Ivy nudged Olivia gently towards the closest picnic table until they were sitting across from each other on the wooden seats, only a few feet away from the forest. Then she reached up to fiddle with something at the back of her neck.

When she brought her hands back down, one of them was cupped protectively around something Olivia couldn't see. 'Look what I brought with me tonight,' she said, opening up her hand.

Olivia leaned across the table, peering at Ivy's hand in the faint moonlight. It took a moment to make out the shape of the small object nestled in Ivy's palm, but then . . . Olivia gasped, reaching out to touch it gently with one finger. 'Your ring!'

Attached to a long golden chain was the emerald ring Ivy had had since she was born: the twin to Olivia's own emerald ring, and the most important, life-long symbol of their sisterhood. They might have been separated as babies and brought up in different families, but their rings had always bound them together, long before they had actually met. From the moment they'd first realised they had matching rings – and discovered exactly what that meant – each girl had kept her own ring safely locked in a jewellery box at home, treasures too precious to ever risk losing.

The sight of Ivy's ring in her hand now brought back every memory Olivia had of all the moments she had spent as a little girl, gazing at her own ring and wondering who her birth family might have been . . . and the precious moment when she had finally realised that she had not just a sister but a *twin*.

Tears filled her eyes. She blinked rapidly, her vision so blurred she barely even noticed the sudden glow in the darkness behind Ivy. Even when the glow transmuted into the shape of a familiar, dark-haired girl, her red dress shining in the darkness and one hand clutching an obsidian bracelet, Olivia couldn't bring herself to feel creeped out.

All she could feel was so much sympathy it was as if her heart might crack.

How could anyone ever bear to lose their twin?

Patience Calhoun's gaze skittered across Olivia and Ivy frantically as she turned her head back and forth, searching desperately around the park. 'Have you seen my sister? Have you seen Hope?'

Olivia let the tears roll down her cheeks as Ivy twisted around to stare at the ghost girl, her mouth falling open. 'I'm so sorry,' Olivia whispered to Patience. 'We were the lucky ones. Our story was the opposite to yours – each finding a twin we never knew we had.'

'That's right.' Ivy's voice sounded choked with emotion as she passed her emerald ring to Olivia. 'And that's why we know exactly what Patience and Hope are feeling – and why Patience can still give Hope her gift after all. The actual bracelet was lost long ago . . . but that's not the important part. When I look at this ring, I don't see a material object. I see a symbol of my favourite person: my twin sister. And what I really want *you* to know – what Patience needs, more than anything, for Hope to know, as her final birthday gift – is just how much it means to us that we found each other.'

'It means everything,' Olivia agreed in a tear-choked whisper.

A burst of cold air swept through the park, coming straight from the forest behind Olivia's back.

'*Aaaaahhhhhhhhhh . . .*'

It was that eerie, wailing wind again – the one that raised every hair on the back of her neck. But as Olivia watched, Patience's face lit up with sudden joy. The ghost girl looked over Olivia's head, directly towards the source of the wind.

Her breath catching in her throat, Olivia turned on her narrow wooden seat, following the ghost's gaze . . .

And saw an identical dark-haired girl in the trees just where the Calhoun house must have once stood. Hope Calhoun wore a wide-skirted dress of pale blue, not red, but her face glowed with happiness, just like her sister's.

The two ghost girls glided towards each other through the air, their faces bright with joy and their feet never touching the ground. Patience held out the bracelet in one hand . . .

. . . and Hope reached out one hand to accept it, wrapping the other around her sister in a hug she had waited more than a century to give.

As Olivia watched, she searched inside herself for any lingering scaredy-cat, freaked-out feelings. She couldn't find a single one. *I'm just so, so happy that they finally found each other again!*

Their pale, shining faces lit up in beaming smiles as they turned to face Ivy and Olivia.

Hope said, 'Thank you for bringing me home to my sister at last.'

'I'm so grateful,' Patience said, her voice thick with emotion.

Ghostly tears sparkled on both of their cheeks, but they were most definitely tears of joy. Olivia sniffled as she watched the two girls link arms and then glide in perfect harmony towards the trees, the site of their old home.

Then they disappeared into the darkness, together.

Olivia scrambled halfway across the table to throw her arms around her sister.

It had never felt better to hug her twin.

Thank darkness that worked, Ivy thought, sighing with pure relief as she hugged Olivia back. 'It's no wonder no one managed to work this one out until now,' she said. She drew back from her sister. 'If I didn't happen to have a twin myself, I'd never have had that crazy idea in the first place!'

'Everything about this situation is a little crazy,' Olivia said ruefully, wiping away the last tears. 'I mean, think about it . . . If my family hadn't moved to Franklin Grove, we'd never have met . . . and if we'd never met, then Hope's ghost might never have been able to return here to be reunited with

Sienna Mercer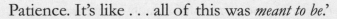

Patience. It's like . . . all of this was *meant to be.'*

With Ivy's keen vampire vision, the darkness was no barrier to glimpsing the strain on her sister's face. 'Uh-oh. Are you feeling totally creeped out right now?'

Laughing a little, Olivia shook her head. 'Oh, I'm not scared any more. Not of them, anyway . . . though I guess I am just a little unnerved by this whole experience.' She shrugged. 'I mean, I know I live in a world where vampires are real, but still – that doesn't make ghosts any less startling when they appear. But as for you . . .!' Jumping up from the table, she reached out one hand to pull Ivy up, too. 'You were amazing, Ivy Holmes! I can't believe you solved that case. Even Sherlock himself couldn't have cracked it!'

Ivy wrapped one arm around her sister's waist. 'How could I not understand what Patience felt? Losing you is the most awful thing I can imagine.' She swallowed hard, blinking back a few tears of her own. 'We need to make each other a promise, OK? Even if we're ever separated somehow, whether it's because you end up travelling the world as a super-famous movie star, or I end up . . . somewhere else . . .'

'Like Transylvania?' Olivia said quietly.

Ivy grimaced. 'I hope not . . . but anyway! We need to promise: no matter how far away from each other we might be, we'll never, ever be estranged. We'll Skype and talk all the time, no matter what.'

'You've got it.' Sniffling again, Olivia drew back, wiping her eyes. As she dropped her hand from her face, though, she gave Ivy a watery grin. 'OK, I think I might have cried about enough for one night . . .'

'Bunny.' Ivy grinned at her sister and bumped shoulders companionably as they started for the park entrance. Olivia bumped her back, then grabbed her hand.

Together, the twins ran for the gate.

At school, three days later, Ivy slid into the seat beside Olivia at their usual cafeteria table for lunch. As she set down her tray and looked around her, she felt a warm glow of satisfaction. Everything was finally back to normal, just the way it was supposed to be. Olivia sat on one side of her and Sophia on the other. Brendan, and Finn and Amelia – or "Famelia", as Olivia always called them – sat opposite.

And for the first time since the Halloween party, Ivy didn't feel a single ounce of stress weighing her down.

Ivy picked up her extra-rare burger and took a big, juicy, delicious bite . . . just as her smartphone dinged with a message.

'Ooh!' She pulled it from her pocket. 'It's Reiko!' she told the others. 'She just sent an email from Japan. Her flight's landed safely, and she says she's glad to be home.'

'Awww.' Olivia leaned over her shoulder, reading the message. 'She also says she misses her new American friends. That's so sweet of her!'

'And I'll tell you guys what's even better.' Ivy grinned triumphantly. 'Reiko says the plane's in-flight entertainment selection had the whole first season of *Shadowtown*. She watched every single episode! She says, "It might be a bit trashy, but it's definitely fun." You see?' She beamed at her friends. 'I'm not the only one who loves that show after all. I've converted someone else, at last!'

Brendan, Sophia, and "Famelia" all groaned.

'Which means it's only fair that you have to watch *Droid Town*!' said Sophia. 'The box set just came in the mail –'

But before she could finish, the whole cafeteria suddenly echoed with the rings and peals of a hundred smartphones all sending alerts at once. With Ivy's phone already open, she got the message first, forwarded on from Penny Taylor, their ex-goth friend.

'Ooohhh . . .' Ivy's jaw dropped open. Then she started to laugh. 'Oh, you guys all have to see this. This is *good*!'

The rest of her friends crowded around her phone as she pressed play on the YouTube preview of an upcoming "blooper" show, *Celebrities' Worst Moments*. The celebrity being exposed in this one was . . .

'Gregor Gleka,' Brendan intoned over Ivy's shoulder, in a throbbing Eastern European accent. 'Caught on film forever, chasing ghosts with a New York accent!' He grinned. 'What a beautiful, beautiful moment.'

But it wasn't Gregor Gleka's spitting, American-accented rage that had gotten the video sent to everyone at their school. It was the five "ghosts" that Gleka was chasing: Josh and his cronies making fools of themselves on-screen, captured for a worldwide audience. Their tinny voices echoed through smartphones all across the cafeteria:

'*Woooooh!*'

'*Wooooooooooh!*'

And there was Garrick, stumbling into everyone else as he ran: 'Hey, I can't see anything!'

As laughter filled the cafeteria, Ivy turned to look for Josh and his greasy pals, bracing herself for their reaction. Would the gang throw a collective tantrum and toss their food against the walls like toddlers? Or would they rise to their feet, scowling in silence, and try to just intimidate everyone out of laughing?

'Unbelievable,' Sophia murmured beside her. 'Just look at them!'

Ivy shook her head.

Josh and his cronies weren't embarrassed at all! Instead, they were grinning right along with everyone else, elbowing each other and doing mock bows for the crowd.

Ivy's keen ears picked out the sound of Josh's smug voice through all the hubbub of the cafeteria as the head of the greasy gang told his friends: 'I *told* you guys we'd be famous!'

She shook her head. 'Maybe they're light-headed from their own stench.'

🦇　　　🦇　　　🦇

Olivia stopped watching the blooper video the moment that a new email alert popped up on her cell phone.

Jackson! Smiling, she opened up his message. It had only been a few days since she'd last seen him, but she already missed her boyfriend. And it looked like he had good news.

Guess what? Your little stunt on Gregor's set went up on YouTube – and our director loves you for it! Eternal Sunset *might not be coming out for a while yet, but you've already gotten it all over the news. Jacob Harker told me to send you at least a dozen roses as a thank you from everyone working on the film!*

Olivia grinned, shaking her head. If only Jackson knew the full story behind that stunt . . .

Then her grin vanished as she read the end of the message:

PS: I won't ask you to do this by email, but next time I see you, I hope you'll be ready to fill me in on all the weirdness that was going on last week. I really want to understand it. XXX

Oh, no. Olivia's chest tightened as she reread that last line again and again.

Jackson had a right to expect some answers. He deserved total honesty from her, too. But what true answers could she possibly give him, without giving away her birth-family's most important secret?

'Olivia?' Ivy nudged her, frowning. 'What's up? Is everything OK?'

Olivia swallowed. 'I'll tell you everything . . . later,' she whispered.

Ivy's frown deepened. 'But . . .'

Tightening her lips, Olivia subtly angled her

216

head in the direction of "Famelia". With non-vamps sitting at their table, there were some things that were never safe to discuss.

She saw understanding dawn on Ivy's face. Her twin's eyes narrowed in a moment of unconcealed concern.

Then Ivy's expression smoothed out. 'Of course,' she whispered. She turned back to the others, holding out her phone and raising her voice. 'Hey, who wants to watch that clip again?'

But even as the rest of her friends laughed and swapped jokes, Olivia couldn't bring herself to join in. The sip she took of her lemonade tasted as flavourless as water as her mind raced with growing panic.

She'd kept her family's secrets for so long . . . but her boyfriend was finally starting to get suspicious.

The fabulous twins had solved one problem . . .

But they might have handed themselves their biggest one yet!

Look out for Ivy and Olivia's 18th fangtabulous adventure!

Coming in 2016

★ ★ ★

Jackson's getting suspicious.
He knows that there's something weird
going on, and he wants answers.

So Olivia must make a big decision.
Keep her boyfriend in the dark, where it's safe,
and risk losing him for good. . .

. . . or reveal the truth?

★ ★ ★

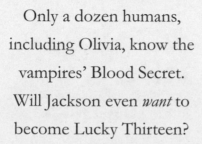

Only a dozen humans,
including Olivia, know the
vampires' Blood Secret.
Will Jackson even *want* to
become Lucky Thirteen?

And is he capable of
passing the Three Trials,
to prove that he can
keep the Secret?

If Jackson fails, his memory
will be erased. He will never remember
his time in Franklin Grove.

And he will never remember Olivia . . .